THE SNAKE TATTOO

Carlotta Caryle Mysteries by Linda Barnes

Trouble of Fools
The Snake Tattoo

THE
SNAKE
TATTOO

LINDA BARNES

A CARLOTTA CARLYLE MYSTERY

ST. MARTIN'S PRESS
NEW YORK

Design by Glen M. Edelstein

Library of Congress Cataloging–in–Publication Data

Barnes, Linda.
    The snake tattoo.
    I. Title.
PS3552.A682S6 1989   813'.54   88-30525
ISBN 0-312-02643-9

First Edition
10 9 8 7 6 5 4 3 2 1

For Richard—
in memory of our daughter

<u>Acknowledgments</u>

Many people have been kind enough to read this novel in various manuscript stages, offering suggested changes and needed encouragement. Chief among them are James Morrow, Karen Motylewski, Richard Barnes, Susan Linn, the ladies who lunch—especially Donnie Sunstein—and Cynthia Mark-Hummel. My thanks to all of them.

I'd also like to express my appreciation to my agent, Gina Maccoby, for her skill, enthusiasm, righteous indignation, and support. Carlotta's honored to have you on her team.

The belief in a supernatural source of evil is not necessary; men alone are quite capable of every wickedness.

—JOSEPH CONRAD
Under Western Eyes,
Part II (1911)

THE SNAKE TATTOO

CHAPTER
1

I shouldn't have taken either case. I certainly shouldn't have taken both. As my mother used to say, in Yiddish more often than English: "You can't ride two horses with one behind."

I was eating dinner—leftover takeout pizza I'd revived with a can of anchovies—when the doorbell rang. I waited, hoping it would ring three times for Roz, but it died after a single bleat. Seems like it only rings when I'm eating.

I grabbed another bite. I was hungry, but I couldn't afford to ignore the bell. Most of my clients make appointments, but I get my share of lost souls clutching the Yellow Pages.

The bell rang again.

"Coming!" I hollered, hoping the prospective client wouldn't mind anchovy-breath. I can't afford to alienate clients. Demand for a female private investigator is picking up, but I still moonlight as a cab driver to afford luxuries like FancyFeast, the only catfood T.C. will eat. I figured keeping the client waiting while I brushed my teeth would offend more than my breath might, so I went to the foyer and started the lengthy process of unlocking, unbarring, and unchaining while squinting through the peephole.

It was Mooney. Lieutenant Mooney of the Boston Police.

Cops on the doorstep don't faze me because I used to be one. In another life I worked for Mooney. Well, really I worked for the fine people of the city of Boston in the Commonwealth of Massachusetts, protecting and defending. But the folks I came into contact with most often—burglars, drunks, druggies, hookers, and abusive spouses—were not the upright citizens who'd hired me. When I used the word "boss," which I hardly ever did since it's a word I hate, I meant Mooney.

I yanked open the door.

"Took you long enough," he said.

"Hey," I said, "you should have flashed your badge. Want some pizza?"

"Anchovies?" he asked, displaying an encyclopedic memory of my eating habits or a good sense of smell.

I nodded.

"Nope," he said.

"I could take the anchovies off," I said, "but you can tell where they've been."

"Yeah," he said. "Looking good, Carlotta."

I was wearing torn jeans and an old gray sweatshirt. My hair was in one of its totally-out-of-control and in-dire-need-of-a-haircut phases so I'd plunked it on top of my head and stuck in a few hairpins. My hair is bright red—natural—and I wished briefly that I'd combed it. I was barefoot, my usual state since size eleven women's shoes are hard to find and difficult to afford. I couldn't remember applying any makeup, and I smelled like an anchovy.

I suppose Mooney's seen me look worse, but he really wasn't paying attention. I probably could have answered the door in lace underwear and he'd have responded with the same preoccupied stare, the same, "Looking good," followed quickly by, "I need to talk to you."

I ushered him into my office, which is really the living room with a rolltop desk.

"Do you mind if—" I started.

"Why don't you bring the pizza in here?" he said.

We do that. Think of the same thing at the same time, I mean. It helped when I worked for him, and sometimes I think he's never forgiven me for leaving the force.

When I got back from the kitchen, balancing two beers and a cardboard round of pizza, I thought I'd see Mooney sprawled on the couch or maybe rocking in the rocking chair. I didn't expect to see him perched on the straightbacked chair next to my desk, the one I reserve for clients.

He minded the beers while I rolled up the desktop and set the pizza on a stack of file folders.

"Pepperoni, too," he said, wrinkling his nose and shaking his head. "You must have Technicolor nightmares."

I grew up in a kosher home, believe it or not. Not that my mom was religious—she was more union organizer than synagogue-goer—but the house we lived in had been my grandmother's, and Mom wouldn't profane her memory by mixing milk and meat there. Outside was a different story, especially at Chinese restaurants, where pork was mysteriously allowable. I don't keep kosher, wouldn't dream of it, but somehow the statute of limitation on kosher has not yet run its course. So *trayf* meat and cheese has the lure of doubly forbidden fruit. I love ham-and-cheese sandwiches and adore pepperoni pizza.

"I could make you a sandwich," I offered.

"I already ate."

Mooney leads a well-regulated life. Aside from a stint in the army and a brief, unsuccessful marriage, he hasn't spent that many nights away from his mom. It's not his fault. His dad died maybe four years ago, and Mom moved straight into Mooney's apartment. That's the way they do it here, the Boston Irish. No personal sacrifice too great. Selfless and charming. Ma probably had meat, potatoes, and two veggies on the table at six sharp every evening.

"When you were a cop," Mooney said carefully, as if he were still deciding how to end the sentence, "did you know a blonde hooker with a snake tattoo?"

"A snake?" I repeated. "Where?"

"Left leg."

"Doesn't ring bells."

"You sure?"

"I'm not up to date on the hooker scene, Mooney. Why do you want this lady?"

"I thought I ought to tell you." He downed most of his beer and then continued reluctantly, "Before you read it in the papers."

I stopped eating, more because of his tone than his words.

"I've been suspended," he said.

I made a noise, said "huh," or "come on," or something. I couldn't believe I'd heard him right. Mooney is the best cop I know. He's sharp enough to make it all the way to police commissioner and decent enough not to want the job. I went to work for him right out of the police academy, and we stuck together for most of my cop career.

"With pay," he said. "Pending investigation."

"Shit," I said.

"I never thought it would happen." He spoke so softly I had to lean forward to hear him. "I thought it would get cleared up right away. They kept it quiet, but it's been three days now so they're giving it to the press. I understand. I mean, if they don't, it'll just leak and look worse than it is." He stared at the beer can logo like he was memorizing it.

"What'll look worse?" I said. "What the hell happened?"

"I thought the department would take care of it, but now I— Shit, I don't know. I think I want to hire you."

I hope my mouth was empty because it must have

dropped open. Yours would have too if you knew what Mooney said about private investigators and other sleazy operators.

The man must have been desperate.

He didn't look desperate. He looked tired. Mooney's eight years older than I am, catching sight of the big four-oh as he puts it, but usually I don't think about his age because his vitality shoves the issue aside. He's a big man, six-four, linebacker weight, with a round face, dark hair, and smart seen-it-all brown eyes. In his button-down shirts and tweed jackets he could pass for a college professor, except for his arms and shoulders. He's got the kind of biceps you don't get from lecturing.

Tonight he had dark smudges under his eyes. His shirt was wrinkled, like he'd slept in it. Part of that was the sag in his shoulders, but I wondered if he'd been ignoring Ma's meals.

I took a bite of pizza and chewed. I never miss a meal if I can help it. Of course my definition of *meal* is loose. Mooney contemplated his Rolling Rock can.

"Want another?" I asked.

"No."

"You gonna tell me about it?"

He studied his fingernails, then the desk, then the room. He's been at my place before, but this time he took stock, registering the worn velvet sofa, the stain on Aunt Bea's favorite rocker, the faint cat-scratches on the mahogany end tables. I'd seen him give crime scenes the same intense once-over. He stood and walked as far as the parakeet's cage, then paced like he was testing the padding under the oriental rug. Finally, he lifted a silver-framed photo off the coffee table.

"How's Paolina?" he asked.

Mention of Paolina makes me smile. It's a reflex action. Mooney knows that, and if he wanted to distract me, he'd found the way. Paolina is my little sister. Not my blood sister; I'm an only child. When I was a cop, I joined this organization, the Big Sisters. They assign you to a girl who needs an older friend, a substitute sister. I got lucky. I got Paolina. She's ten and a half now. It's been over three years since I fell for that scared skinny face and those huge dark eyes.

"Good picture," he said.

"I got a letter yesterday," I said. "I was starting to worry."

Starting to worry, hah. I was close to panic by the time the letter arrived from Bogota. It had plenty of stamps on it, not to mention a boldly printed ENTREGA IMMEDIATA, which made me think the post office should have taken less than three weeks to deliver it. I didn't have to take it out of my pocket to remember what it said.

Dear Carlotta,

Paolina's bilingual, but she sticks to English with me. Her handwriting is messy and her spelling is often unusual. She'd made a real effort, drawn lines on the paper to keep her sentences straight, and then tried to erase them, blurring some of the words.

The airplane was fun and scary. Bogota is crowded. There are cows that walk in the street, and chickens. The man they call my grandfather is very sick. I miss you.

Love ya,
Paolina

"She's okay," I said to Mooney. "But I don't know when she'll be back."

Marta, Paolina's crazy Colombian mother, had called me five weeks ago. Her father was sick in Bogota and she needed to see him before he died. And she had to take Paolina, her oldest, because Popi would remember Paolina. I didn't get more detail because Marta doesn't speak much English and my Spanish is poor.

I've spent a lot of time replaying that conversation. As far as I know Marta and her family don't get along. She hasn't spoken to or about them for as long as I've known her. Maybe money was involved, an inheritance. That would account for Marta's insistence on bringing Paolina. One look at that kid and I'd sign my millions over to her, if I had them. I'm prejudiced, I admit.

Paolina exacted two promises before she left. One: that I'd continue to drill the parakeet in Spanish. Paolina and I have an ongoing argument about the bird. She belonged to my late Aunt Bea, who named her Fluffy in some lapse of creative spirit. When I inherited house and bird, I renamed the budgie immediately. She is now Red Emma, after the infamous anarchist of the twenties. Emma Goldman was one of my mom's heroes, one of mine too. Paolina doesn't like the name because, as she rightly points out, Red Emma is not red, but green. So Paolina calls her Esmeralda.

The budgie, less than clever on its best days, has stopped speaking entirely in its confusion.

The other promise was that I wouldn't get another little sister while she was gone. The thought never entered my head. Paolina's my little sister no matter where she is.

"She'll be back," Mooney said softly.

"Hey, sorry," I said.

"I think I'd better tell you now."

While I'd been dreaming of Paolina, he must have tossed some kind of mental coin. It had teetered on its edge, then come down in my favor. He replaced Paolina's photo on the coffee table, strolled back, and sat down.

I waited.

"It was Saturday night," he began, shifting into the voice he used for reading reports and giving orders. "I stopped off for a drink on the way home. At the Blue Note."

He glanced at me, but I kept my face carefully blank. The Note is a Combat Zone bar, a fleabag pick-up joint where hookers congregate.

Not that he owed me any explanation. Mooney and I have never been an item. We've gotten damn close, but I always back off. I've been married, I've played the field, and I consider myself retired from the man-woman business. To tell you the truth, I can't figure it out at all.

"I had a drink," Mooney continued. "A draft beer, and I ordered another. This woman—well, she came on to me. I wasn't on duty or anything. I hadn't seen her around. I figure she's new talent. Young. Runaway. Vietnamese, so I'm trying to remember words and phrases I picked up over there, but I can't remember much. Hell, who wants to remember? She didn't push it, didn't make any hard offers. The come-on was like a dating bar or something. If she'd gone any further I would have had to identify myself, but I don't think I'd have busted her. I'd have warned her not to cozy up to men who wear shiny black lace-up shoes."

I grinned at his description of cop footwear, but I didn't say anything because Mooney seemed to be giving his report to the mantel clock. I chewed softly, not wanting to remind him I was in the room.

"I was talking with her," he went on, "just talking, and some guy grabs me by the shoulder and tosses me halfway across the room. When I got myself sorted out, the next thing I know the guy is yelling at the woman, and I figure it's her pimp, and he's made me for a cop, and he's mad at her. I should have realized if he'd known I was a cop, he wouldn't have yanked me off her like that. . . ."

He reached over and took a slice of pizza, carefully removing the anchovies and resettling them on an adjacent piece. I nodded to show it was okay. Double anchovies would be fine with me, and there was plenty of pizza for both of us. For two minutes, chewing was the loudest sound in the room.

"He starts shaking the girl around," Mooney said. "Not hitting, but threatening her. So I get in the middle and he pulls a blade. I identify myself as a cop. I mean, I definitely remember saying, in the middle of all this crap, 'Boston Police, put down your weapon,' and feeling like a total jerk. He doesn't act like he hears me. I lose any Vietnamese I ever had. I draw my gun, but no way I'm gonna shoot. Too tight, other people around. The bastard comes at me. We move around a lot, knock some glasses off the bar. People are hollering and racing around, but all I can focus on is that damn hand and that knife. He gets in close, but he's not a good fighter. Still, he keeps coming. He misses me by a mile and I smack him with the gun butt. He goes down. I cuff him and read Miranda. And the rest goes by the book."

"Sounds okay," I ventured after a long pause. I wondered if Mooney hadn't come to me earlier because it was about picking up a woman. "Sounds like a good bust."

Mooney made a sound that should have been a laugh but there wasn't any humor in it. "The guy's skull cracked. He's in New England Medical Center and he's in bad shape. He's a goddamn leader of the Dorchester Vietnamese community. The woman, the girl I thought was the runaway hooker, that's his wife. She swears he didn't have a blade. Nobody saw a knife except me, and there wasn't one on him when they took him to the hospital, and nobody found one in the bar. They say he hardly speaks English. And nobody in the bar saw a freaking thing. Not the bartender, not the drunks. They're calling it excessive brutality right now, but it could get worse if he . . ."

"Dies?" I said, when Mooney's voice trailed off.

"Yeah," he said. "Dies."

I eased out of my chair, went to the kitchen, and popped the tops off two cans: one beer, one Pepsi. I put the beer on the desk. Mooney took a long drink.

"You know, Carlotta," he said, "I've run through this thing in my mind so often, sometimes I think I must be going nuts. I go over it and over it and it never seems to change, but then when BPS asks me about it I feel like I'm on the other side of a mirror or something, or I'm speaking another language."

BPS is the Bureau of Professional Standards. Also known as Internal Affairs.

"I'm sorry," I said, because I didn't know what else to say.

"I keep thinking about the newspapers, Carlotta. I mean, with all the troubles the department's been having lately, they'll rip my hide. It won't be my case in particular. Hell, I'll get to represent all the rotten cops in this rotten city. Everybody on the goddamn city council will have an opinion on this. The mayor. Every goddamn candidate for public office. I'll be a racist and a fascist and God knows what the hell else."

He was right. It was not a great time for a cop to draw attention to himself. The Boston Police are no better and no worse than any others, but lately the newspapers have been unfolding scandal after scandal. First came the revelation that cops pulled the multimillion-dollar Medford Trust bank robbery. Then came the assorted confessions of said cops, men who seemed incapable of shutting up once granted immunity. Among other daring deeds, they'd stolen copies of police civil service exams. They'd broken into headquarters, elevated grades for their buddies and lowered them for guys they didn't like. The press called it "Examscam." Now there were rumors that cops were taking payoffs to "protect" bars, and worse, leaving them unprotected. The newshounds hadn't come up with a catchy slogan for it yet, but something with "gate" or "scam" in it was bound to surface soon.

"So," Mooney said, blowing out a deep breath, "I was hoping you'd know this witness. She must have seen the whole thing. Bleached-blonde. Hooker. Good shape, but not a young chickie. What I remember most is she had a tattoo, a snake. It was twisting up her leg, starting at the ankle, and she was wearing a short leather skirt."

"Shouldn't be too hard to find," I said. "A snake tattoo."

"That's what I thought. I was sure Vice would nail her right off, or at least have her in the files. They've got rosebuds, hearts, dirty words, and butterflies, but no snakes. And nobody seems to know her. And now I'm out of it. I can't even check what's going on, who's looking for her. I'm completely out."

I said, "Notice anybody else?"

"She's the one I remember most. The barkeep was a sandy-haired guy with a big gut. There weren't a whole lot of others. You know bar people. The minute they see a cop, they melt into the woodwork."

There was a loud bang from upstairs. It was a sound to which I was growing accustomed.

"Roz doing karate?" Mooney asked. This was not a smartass remark. Roz, my tenant, is a devotee of the martial arts, not to mention the martial arts instructor.

"Plumbers," I said as the banging continued.

"Trouble?"

"Remodeling the bathroom."

"Business must be good."

I let him think that. There was more rumbling and thudding from above. It sounded like God bowling.

"So what about it?" he said.

"You need her, I'll find her, Mooney."

"Okay, then," he said, managing to sound both apprehensive and relieved. He leaned to one side to slip his wallet out of his hip pocket. "A hundred do for a retainer?"

"On the house," I said.

"You take a check?"

"Read my lips, Mooney. On the house."

"I'm not a charity case."

"I'm not offering handouts. Favor for favor, like always."

"That was when you were a cop."

"Same thing."

"This is too big for a favor," he said.

"Want to bet on it?" I said. Betting is an old tradition with Mooney and me. Another thing we have in common: We both hate to lose. "When's the hearing?"

"The twenty-sixth. Two weeks from today."

"If I find her before your cop buddies do—and before the hearing—you pay. If I don't find her, or I don't find her first, it's a freebie."

"Look, Carlotta, I have every confidence in the force—"

"Sure you do," I said.

"No bet," he said. "I pay, whether you find her or not."

Mooney doesn't earn big bucks. And his mom gets a pittance from Social Security.

"Look," I said, "if you thought the cops were going to find her first you wouldn't be here, right?"

The pipes rumbled threateningly.

"Right," he said gloomily. "Like I said, I thought Vice would nab her in twenty-four hours, but now—"

"So trust your hunches, Moon. It's what makes you a good cop."

He almost smiled. I guess nobody'd called him a good cop for a while.

"Well, if we're talking about a bet here," he said with

more spirit, "then let's raise the ante. If you find her first, I pay whatever you private cops extort these days. But if you don't find her first—and I'm not in jail—you, uh, go out with me. A real date, not an ice cream cone."

When I was a cop, Mooney and I worked together so well I wouldn't even consider dating him. Now that I'm private, no longer a link in his chain of command, he asks me out a lot. And I always refuse. Somewhere along the line I decided he was too good a friend to risk on romance.

Or maybe I just hear my mother's voice. "Never get involved with a cop," was another of her favorite sayings. She married one—my dad—so she knew what she was talking about.

"How about you pay me in ice cream cones?" I said.

"Seriously," he said. "A date."

"Let's keep this a commercial transaction, okay?" I said.

"Then no bet. I pay you for your time."

"Then I don't take the damn case."

"Come on, Carlotta. What have you got to lose?"

"Not my virginity, Moon. How'd your mom feel about that?"

"I'll ask her first thing when I get home, Carlotta."

"Look, Mooney." I bit the inside of my cheek to keep from laughing. According to Mooney, his mom has no sense of humor, period. "Let me do this my way. I don't need your money up front. I'm not starving. I'm doing okay. I've got a roof over my head, a paying tenant."

Even free plumbing help. I didn't mention that because it didn't feel like an advantage.

"Face it," Mooney said, "you're not making a living, Carlotta. You drive that dumb cab nights. It's dangerous."

"I like driving that dumb cab."

Mooney is stubborn and I'm stubborner. We went at it for a while and finally left the terms of the agreement undecided. He insisted on signing one of my standard client forms, and I let him.

I figured I could always rip it up.

CHAPTER
2

If it hadn't been for Twin Brothers Plumbing Company, I'd have tucked myself into bed soon after Mooney left. As it happened, two hours later, I found myself slouched in the driver's seat of a Green & White cab, peering down a Combat Zone alley, trying not to freeze to death. Just yesterday Boston had rewarded the faithful with a whopping April snowstorm that was making the natives reconsider California. Not me. I'd rather shovel out the daffodils than put up with crystal-gazing neighbors and the odd earthquake or two.

Spring flowers did not brighten up my alleyway. I was parked near its mouth, close to a fire hydrant. The narrow roadbed was decorated with smashed wine bottles, greasy hamburger wrappings, and piles of slushy snow. I hugged my arms and wished for a warmer coat while I scanned the rickety staircase-cum-fire-escape of a three-story yellow brick flophouse. Back when I was a cop assigned to the Zone, a pimp named Renney housed his stable there. One of his fillies was Janine. And I needed to find her, to check if my hunch was right.

I shifted my rear end. Gloria, the formidable dispatcher at G&W, didn't hand out the comfy new cabs with the bucket seats to last-minute jockeys. She'd given me the best hack available on short notice at 10:37 P.M. I was doing Bostonians a favor by taking it out of circulation for a few hours.

See, as soon as Mooney left, I raced upstairs to check on the plumbers. Big mistake.

Let me tell you about Twin Brothers Plumbing Company.

Twin Brothers is not run by twin brothers or any kind of brothers. One guy is black, one white; one short, one tall. Both dumb. George, possibly the dumber one, had hired me two months ago to investigate a rash of company thefts. He hadn't read about my finer qualities in the newspapers or been referred by my buddies on the Boston Police. He hadn't even seen my big red ad in the Yellow Pages. Roz sent him.

Roz, a punk-rock artist, dwells in the attic of my old Victorian house in two semifinished rooms that she's painted a charming matte black. Her living room has kitschy furniture and five television sets; her bedroom is totally decorated in tumbling mats. Roz does karate, extremely weird acrylics, and dyes her hair a new color every week. She also handles the housework. In exchange for the latter she gets a vastly reduced rent on a place within spitting distance of Harvard Square.

When Roz fixed me up with a client I should have smelled trouble.

Now I don't screen customers for smarts because, quite frankly, my clients are not so plentiful that I turn them away in droves. Two months ago I'd been truly pleased to see George at my door, eager to hear about his missing U-pipes, wrenches, and snakes.

I staked out Twin Brothers Plumbing for eleven frigid nights before George's teenage cousin decided to help himself to some copper pipes. I'd intended to just take pictures, but the kid was slight, shorter than I am, and didn't look spunky enough to fight back. So I tackled him with one of my best volleyball leaps, only to discover I'd underestimated him. The jerk struggled, grabbed a fistful of my hair, and poked me in the eye. I held on, subdued his youthful enthusiasm with a few yards of rope, and introduced him to the gents he'd been stealing blind. That's where the trouble should have ended. Kudos all around and a fat paycheck, right? Instead, that's where the trouble began.

See, George didn't want me to catch a member of the family. George had his heart set on the entrapment of one Elisha Johnson, some poor SOB employee who hadn't done anything wrong except make eyes at George's sister. And it was about then that I discovered Twin Brothers Plumbing was so far in the red that catching their thief was not going to help. Bankruptcy loomed, and I was last on a long list of creditors. It looked like I was going to have to take my paltry advance and chalk up the rest to experience.

But George, the tall dumb white guy with the sister, and Rodney, his short coffee-colored partner, were honest in their fashion. They offered to work off their debt in trade. An irresistible offer, right—especially if you've priced plumbing help lately. I mean, who can't use a plumber? I accepted eagerly because my old Victorian is long on charm and location, and short on convenience. My upstairs toilet gurgles, the sink is chipped and cracked, the bathtub is designed for a midget, and the floor, far from being level, collects dust puppies in the back corner. I had visions of gleaming tile, tasteful wallpaper. Hell, maybe a Jacuzzi.

And now I was learning, firsthand, why Twin Brothers Plumbing went broke.

I had specified beige tile. The tile they showed up with was so dark brown it was practically black. I wanted one of those pedestal sinks. They had a boxy number, complete with cabinet, in, I kid you not, Day-Glo orange.

Now I'm good at saying no. But I hadn't reckoned with Roz. Roz is not just a tenant. She is my sometime assistant, and, more importantly, my housecleaner. I need her. I can't stand housework. Because she's an artist, albeit the punk variety, and because I was grateful she'd steered clients my way even though they turned out to be almost deadbeats, I'd assured her that she could work with the Twin Brothers on redesigning the bathroom.

I should have realized, once I'd seen the guys, that whatever judgment Roz possessed couldn't be trusted.

Roz has basically lamentable taste in men; that is, she judges them purely by exterior charms. A good bod is all to Roz, so it's not hard to guess how she became acquainted with the Twin Bros. George, the tall guy, has muscles, or at least he looks like he's got muscles until you see Rodney, the short guy, who's really got muscles. Both of them won Roz's nonmonogamous heart and her artistic sense, such as it is, succumbed.

That the two brothers are both married, each to a woman named Marie, hopefully not the same woman named Marie, makes little difference to Roz. Me, I never mess with the married kind. Life is tough enough.

A shadow moved on the window overlooking the fire escape, and I straightened up. It was a skinny gray cat whose eyes caught the glare from the window and lit up like emergency flashers.

I relaxed my grip on the steering wheel and unclenched my teeth. Just thinking about Twin Brothers Plumbing can do that to me. I decided that storming out of the house had been a wise move. Otherwise I'd have tossed the tile (still the wrong color), the sink (a new weird avocado shade), and the two stooges out the bathroom window. Maybe they'd have landed in a snowdrift. Maybe not.

I huddled deeper into the folds of my inadequate coat. If I'd thought about more than escape, I'd have grabbed my parka instead of my old wool peacoat. I jammed my hands into my pockets. No gloves.

If I'd gone back for gloves, I'd have fired them. If I'd fired them, I'd have had to live with an unfinished bathroom—no toilet, no sink, no bathtub—for eternity. If I'd fired them, I'd be sorry. Sorrier. I was already sorry I'd ever heard of Twin Brothers Plumbing.

The left front window of the cab didn't quite close, so a gale blew into my ear. The heater was so feeble a blanket in the back seat was standard issue. Since the cab had the required-by-Boston-law dividing shield, the only way I could snatch the blanket was to get out, open the back door, and generally draw attention to myself. So far, I'd resisted. Every half-hour I fired up the engine, eked out a little heat, and got by on that. I tried to think warm thoughts.

A cab is a good surveillance vehicle, almost but not quite on a par with a telephone company van. People don't pay much attention to cabs unless they need one, and hailers only pay attention to cabs that stop. Pedestrians and other drivers expect cabbies to be rude, erratic, and apt to make sudden U-turns. Cabs blend into the background.

Behind the wheel of a cab I blend into the background too, which can be a challenge for a six-foot-one-inch redhead who's thin enough to make every inch count. Driving, I wear an old slouch cap that hides my hair, and since I'm sitting down, people don't make comments about the quality of the air up here. "My, you're tall for a woman," people tell me when I'm standing, as if I might not have noticed otherwise.

I like driving a cab. It got me through college without waitressing and taught me how to get around the city without ever stopping for a red light. Late nights on the streets of Boston, I feel at home. I get off on finding the fastest shortcut, the quickest bypass. After graduation, I gave up cabbing for police work. I liked that too, but I had trouble taking orders. I wound up getting fired.

Well, that's not exactly true. They let me resign. If it hadn't been for Mooney, I'd have been fired.

From the mouth of my alley I could see the main drag, Washington Street, where stall-and-crawl traffic prevailed, much of it slow because the gents inside the BMWs and Volvos were trolling for hookers. Business is down because of AIDS, but business goes on.

Much of my least favorite cop time was spent in the Zone. I was in great demand because none of the guys wanted to wear heels and play hooker. God, I hated decoy patrol. Aping a lady of the night and arresting some poor slob who wanted his sex on a pay-as-you-go basis was not why I'd joined the force.

A lean black hooker made her way up the fire escape into Renney's place. She was wearing heels so high the tendons on her legs stood out like cords, and a skirt so short it disappeared under her leather jacket. I couldn't remember her name. I thought I'd seen her before. Mitzi, maybe.

I wasn't absolutely sure Janine would turn up at Renney's. I wasn't even sure Janine was the one. But sometime between Mooney's departure and the moment I slammed out my front door, Janine had sprung to mind.

Janine used decals. Rinse-off tattoos. Vegetable coloring. She used to say guys would pay extra for a tattooed woman, but they also craved variety, so tattoos of the evening were her specialty. She used to design some pretty elaborate ones, and that snake sounded like Janine to me. And back when I used to arrest her, say, twice every three months, she homed to Renney.

So why not dial Mooney and give him the information? Because Mooney and I have a complicated history of debits and credits, and I hate it when he's one up in the favors department. Why not call any cop and tell him how to help one of his own? Because I would like the PD to owe me a big one. If I handed them Janine on a platter, saved Mooney from the disgrace of a hearing, maybe they'd tell a few lawyers what a good evidence hunter I am, what a dogged tailer, et cetera. The old boy network operates here in full strength.

Also, I hadn't seen Janine in maybe a year and a half. The life of a street hooker is short and brutal, and for all I knew Janine was now a suburban mother of two. I didn't want the cops to share a giggle at my expense.

So I watched the fire escape. I waited. I saw two plainclothes cops arrest a lady who looked too old to be selling her body and a boy who looked too young to know he had something to sell. I saw glassine packets slip into chino pockets, and folding money fold itself very small and disappear. Somebody tossed a beer bottle out a window. But no Janine.

I was resting my head on the headrest, practically unconscious, when the door opened, the back seat creaked, the door slammed, and a male voice, young by the cracking adolescent sound, said, "Please! Drive."

Maybe it was the youthfulness, maybe the urgency. Whatever, I bit back my off-duty reply and drove.

I took two quick rights because the traffic opened up that way and the kid seemed to be ducking down in the cab like he didn't want anybody to see him. I hoped I wasn't participating in a robbery. Bank robbers seldom take cabs, but after my experience as a cop, nothing would surprise me.

I adjusted the rearview mirror so I could see my fare.

He was huddled in a corner, legs pressed tightly together, hands balled into fists on his thighs. I took a long look at his face, memorizing it for a potential police artist sketch. I've made that a practice ever since the first time I was robbed by a fare.

He couldn't have been more than sixteen. His face was long and thin and practically blue from cold. His eyes were close together under a bony ridge of brow and were so deep set it was hard to tell their color. I decided on gray, like pale stones. His nose was thin too, jutting out like a beak, giving him a faintly arrogant air offset by ears that stuck out too far. His hair was cornsilk blond, kind of wispy, a little bit punk. He wore black jeans, a T-shirt, and a thin windbreaker, not much for April winter. He'd probably grow into his height in a couple years, but for now his hands were outsize and his chest practically concave. He was shivering, but he hadn't touched the blanket.

I reached back and opened the talk square in the shield, thinking I'd tell him to wrap up.

"Damn," he was saying quietly. "Goddamn, goddamn, goddamn." The litany trailed off, then he looked around, suddenly aware of his surroundings, got a new note of panic in his voice, and said, "Pull over, okay?"

We hadn't traveled more than eight blocks. I parked underneath a streetlamp. I maintain that people are less likely to rob you under streetlamps. I'm a firm believer in them.

He was quiet for so long I turned around. He seemed to be searching through his pockets, patting his shirt, pants. He turned the pockets of his windbreaker inside out and stared at the lining in disbelief that was either real or well-counterfeited. "Damn," he said again, loudly, explosively. "Look, I don't have any money, but if you could take me home, trust me for it, I can pay you when I get there. Honest, I'm good for it." His eyes were red. It might have been from the cold or he might have been crying. Through the shield I couldn't tell.

"Where's home?" I asked.

"Lincoln."

Lincoln is about as far from the Combat Zone as you can get. Not in miles—it's less than an hour away—but in character. Lincoln's a ritzy little bedroom suburb. Clean, fresh, perfect. The lawns are manicured. The leash law is of burning concern at town meetings. The churches are white with steeples. The populace is white with 2.4 kids, healthy collies, and Volvo wagons. The garbage fairy takes the compacted trash to the dump without dirtying the winding streets.

"Look," I said, "If you got robbed, maybe you want to report it to the cops?" I was thinking that Lincoln was a long drive and Janine was not going to amble into my cab while I was on the road.

"I'll pay you, really. My folks will."

"You sure they're home?" I didn't want the thirty-mile trek out to Lincoln. I wanted Janine.

He folded his arms, sank back on the seat, and looked longingly at the blanket. He was at that age where he couldn't admit he was cold enough to need it. "I'm pretty sure they're home. If they're not I could, like, write you a check or something, or borrow it from the neighbors."

He felt around in his pockets some more, said "damn" a few more times, and then said, "I can't believe this. I really can't believe this."

"Look," I said, "Did you get rolled?"

"Rolled?" he said.

"By a hooker? Get your wallet stolen, you know?"

He blushed to the roots of his hair. Then he tried to act cool, like he picked up hookers all the time.

"No, it's not that. Really." He stared around the cab

some more, not looking at the blanket. "Well, I don't know. Look, maybe if there's a police station near here . . . Well, at least I could call somebody to come and get me."

"There's a station," I said. "Maybe you should tell the cops about your wallet."

I started driving toward New Sudbury Street. It was a hell of a lot closer than Lincoln.

The kid spoke when we were almost there. "Do you think the police could help if it's, uh, personal? Like somebody I need to find, somebody missing, a friend . . ."

"A friend stole your wallet?"

"I think I, uh, I must have dropped it or something," he said. "Yeah, while I was standing on the corner, it must have just dropped out of . . ."

While he babbled, I took a card from my purse and stuck it in the tray in the dividing shield. I had to tap on the shield to get him to pick it up. He was still patting at his clothes in disbelief.

"What's this?" he said when he'd read the card at least twice. I could see his eyes move in the mirror.

"What it says. I'm an investigator. If the police can't find your friend, maybe I can. The cops have lots of missing people to look for. I specialize."

He studied the card and me. I tried to look sober and responsible.

I stopped in front of the police station. "Ask for Detective Royce," I said. "And if they don't turn up anything, my number's on the card."

He sat there shivering for a while, then he said he was sorry he couldn't pay me. He asked what the fare was. I read him the meter, and he said he would mail me the $3.55, plus tip. He opened the door.

"Do you have a dime so you can call home?" I asked. "Get somebody to pick you up?"

He just sat there with the door open. Red-eyed. He reminded me of a boy I'd had a crush on in the tenth grade. What was his name? Doug somebody?

I reached in my purse and pulled out a five, passed it through the hatch.

"Hey," he said.

"Add it to what you already owe me," I said. "They've got a sandwich machine."

"I'm hungry," he said like he'd just realized it. He held the bill up and smiled, a flash of nice white teeth. Even teeth, like you get from wearing braces for years. "Thanks a lot."

"Don't drink the coffee and you'll be fine," I said.

Then he disappeared in the gloom.

CHAPTER
3

I wasted another two hours in the Zone—watching Renney's place, cruising the bus station, checking Renney's flat again—without catching so much as a glimpse of Janine. Any one of twenty shivering streetwalkers, high-booted against the cold, could have sported a python underneath her opaque pantyhose. So I quit, returned the cab, hurried home, brushed my teeth, slid between the sheets, and discovered I wasn't sleepy after all.

I have periodic bouts of insomnia. It's not fatal and that's the best I can say for it. I used to lie there and curse, but I've learned to cope. Now I get out of bed, pretend it's morning, and do something I enjoy, like fooling with my old National Steel guitar.

I tried a Blind Lemon Jefferson tune in E, one from the first Biograph album. I can still finger some pretty decent blues riffs, but I don't practice like I used to, so I don't sound the way I should. I had to repeat the bridge three times till I got the timing right.

I like to hear a harmonica in the background, or maybe a thumping bass line. My ex-husband played bass, and guitar, mandolin, fiddle, banjo—anything with strings. I miss the harmonies, but I've just about stopped missing him. I imagine the harmony, or sometimes I play along with my tape deck. I don't do much modern stuff. No love songs. Just old-time done-me-wrong blues.

My fingers found a melody. I remembered the words:

> Cocaine's for horses, not for men,
> Doctor said it'd kill me, but he didn't say when.
> Cocaine, running 'round my brain.

That was one of my ex's favorites, the way Chris Smither used to do it, fine and loose and lazy. Cal used to sing it doped to the gills, like a lung cancer patient gulping cigarette smoke.

I sang it through, tried a key change.

My voice is not great, but it's true, a gift of perfect pitch. With all the windows in my cab shut, I wail and shout along with the radio—whenever I don't have a fare. At home I really pull out the volume stops. I used to worry about Roz, but so far I haven't discovered a noise loud enough to wake her. Mainly she disturbs me.

See, Roz makes noise when Roz makes love, and

even over my guitar, I could hear her scream and moan. I admit to my share of curiosity, so when I heard the steps creak about four-thirty, I stuck my head out to investigate.

It was the taller of the Twin Brothers, sneaking down the stairs, zipping his jeans. At that moment I gave up all hope for my bathroom.

CHAPTER
4

I must have just nodded off when the doorbell chimed. My subconscious knocked the phone off the hook, but the damn thing kept ringing and pretty soon I figured it was probably the door. It could have been three rings for Roz, but I hadn't been counting and I knew she'd never hear it anyway, so I grabbed my bathrobe and pelted downstairs barefoot.

If it was one of the Twin Brothers I was planning to strangle him.

As a courtesy to the burglars I always keep my porch light burning. With my right eye pressed against the peephole, I could make out a figure on the front stoop.

While I groped for the dangling ends of my bathrobe belt, found them, and tied them tightly around my waist, the thin shape turned to face the door. It was the kid I'd dropped off at the police station.

I'd told him to mail me the fare, not special-deliver it in the middle of the night.

"I'm sorry," he said as soon as I yanked open the door, before I could get in a word. It takes the wind out of my sails when somebody apologizes before I get a chance to blow up.

He winced as he spoke, and lifted a hand to his face. A thin trickle of blood oozed from the corner of his mouth. His lips were puffy; a dark seam split the lower one.

"You ought to put an ice cube on that," I said.

"I'm sorry, really." He took a long look at my robe, and gave his head a quick shake as if he were waking from a trance. "What time is it? Oh geez, oh shit, you were sleeping. I didn't know what time it was. . . . I wanted to hire you. I mean, I didn't just come because somebody—" He lifted his hand to his mouth. "Because of this."

"You better come in," I said, hoping to shut the door before the wind blew open my robe. The kid seemed frozen on the front porch. I practically had to pry his hand off the storm door and tug him into the kitchen. I put some ice cubes in a dish towel, gave him the resulting ice pack, and sat him down in a chair.

The cat strolled in, wide awake, and nuzzled the kid's ankles. T.C., a large black cat with a white forepaw, usually competes with other males, of any species. Perhaps he considered this one too young. Out of combat, so to speak.

The kid was incredibly polite. He kept telling me not to bother while I hauled out the iodine. He "pleased" and "thank-you'd" and patted the cat, who proceeded to make an exhibition of himself. You know, the whole nobody-in-this-house-ever-petted-me-before routine. Rolling over. Purring shamelessly. The kid asked if he should be quiet so as not to wake anybody else, with a kind of speculative air that wondered if I were married, sleeping alone, or what. Maybe he wasn't that young. I thought about Roz and the Twin Brother who'd exited at four-thirty. I told him not to worry about the noise.

"I'd like to hire you," the kid said, his words blurred through towel and ice. "To investigate. Like on the card. You do that, right?"

I sank into one of my mismatched kitchen chairs, the one with the split vinyl seat, and made a reassuring noise to contrast with my appearance. My bathrobe is not recommended interviewing-a-prospective-client-wear; it looks like a bright red chenille bedspread, stitched together on the sides. I love red, but I don't usually wear it in public because it clashes with my hair.

Under the robe I was wearing a white singlet T-shirt, which is my favorite nightwear because it's soft and doesn't scratch. I got in the habit of wearing my husband's T-shirts to bed when I was married. No matter what alluring nightie I started out in, by the middle of the night I'd give up and go back to the old reliables. Lace itches. When we split up he left me a drawerful. I threw them out and bought replacements. It didn't seem right to get rid of Cal and keep his shirts.

I adjusted the robe over my crossed knees. Usually when I'm interviewing a client, I dress okay, nothing fancy, but okay. There I sat, 5:22 A.M., in my beat-up bathrobe, feeling like the "before" illustration in a "Dress for Success" manual.

On the other hand, the kid's appearance made his plea for help seem urgent. His jeans were muddy, his shirt torn. He said "excuse me" before he headed to the tiny half-bath to tend his lip in privacy. When he returned his face was pale but his hair was neatly combed. He'd probably been careful not to bleed in the sink.

It didn't seem right to tell him to come back at nine just so I could dress up.

"Look," he said, "I need to find this girl, Valerie Haslam." That much came out clear and strong. Then his voice started to falter, and he sat down and addressed the tabletop. "She's, she's this girl I know. We go to the same school. She's, like, lived across the street from me forever . . . and we're, like, friends, you know."

"Maybe you should tell me your name," I said, handing him a fresh ice cube.

"Shit, I mean, excuse me, I forgot. I'm Jeremy, Jerry, I mean, Jeremy's a dumb name. My friends call me Jerry. Jerry Toland." He stuck out the hand that had been holding the ice pack. I almost screamed when I shook it, it was so cold.

"Valerie isn't, like, the kind of girl who runs away, I mean who just takes off and doesn't say anything. I mean, she'd have said good-bye or something. But everybody says she hasn't been gone long, and maybe she just left on her own, and girls that age are more mature, and maybe she went to New York for the week. I mean, they don't seem all that interested, you know, like she's one more missing piece of luggage. Her mom's not home, and the guidance counselor says it's none of my business. I guess I could have gone to the Lincoln Police, but she's not in Lincoln anymore, and I can't see those guys doing anything real, you know, about getting her back."

"How old are you, Jerry?" I said.

He bristled. "What's that got to do with it?"

"How old?"

"Look, do me a favor. Don't tell me how it will be all better when I'm older and that shit. I mean you can't be that much older than I am, so don't bother telling me that shit."

Every time the kid swore, he looked at me to see if I was going to faint. When he said *shit* it came out like it had quotation marks around it. Maybe he'd decided to swear as proof of his advanced age. He should hear the ten-year-olds at Paolina's housing project.

"It's about contracts, Jerry," I said. "I do what I do for a living, to pay my bills."

"Well, don't worry about that," he said. "I've got money. I mean, I couldn't pay my cab fare but that's because my wallet—" He swallowed. "Because I lost my wallet. I've got a goddamned bank account, stocks, bonds, Christ, you name it. Money's what I've got."

"How old are you?"

"Why?"

"We could do this all night."

"I'm seventeen," he said bitterly. His tone surprised me. I guess I think when you're seventeen you should be pleased to admit it. I guess I hope when I'm seventy-nine, I'll be pleased to admit it.

I said, "In this state any contract you sign is not binding. You can pull out any time and there I am, looking for Valerie."

He offered his hand again, the cold one, and looked me defiantly in the eye. "My name is Jerry Toland. I live at 112 Lilac Palace Drive, Lincoln. I want to hire you. I'm not going to back out of this, and if you won't do it, tell me the name of somebody who will."

I liked the way he said it, but I didn't let on. I said, "And you'll wake him up, too?"

"Shit. I am sorry about that, really I am. I mean, I apologize and everything."

"How's your mouth?"

"It's okay. The ice helps."

"How'd it happen?"

"I was stupid."

I liked that, too. No excuses. No complaints. So I said, "My office is in the living room. My desk, anyhow. Why don't you come in there and we'll talk about it."

"Even if I'm only seventeen?" he said.

"Even if you're only sixteen, which I suspect."

"Sixteen and seven months." He tried out a grin but his lip wouldn't cooperate.

I went back into the living room for the second time in twenty-four hours, which probably broke some kind of record. Usually I only go in there to feed Fluffy—I mean, Red Emma—and I only keep her out of respect for my Aunt Bea. The bird cage used to have pride of place in front of the bay window. I moved it to one side so it doesn't block the view of the magnolia tree on the tiny pocket of front lawn.

I've never redecorated the living room, so it still looks

the way it did when Aunt Bea died. Well, almost. Aunt Bea used to work up a real shine on the mahogany. Roz flicks a dust cloth at it when the spirit moves her, which is my kind of cleaning. I suppose I ought to take better care of things, but I still have trouble believing the house is mine. I pay my real estate taxes monthly, into an escrow account. That way it feels like rent and, believe me, the rent's getting steeper all the time.

I do most of my work at the kitchen table because I like the view of the refrigerator. But clients seem to prefer Aunt Bea's decor.

I led Jerry into the living room and turned on the desk lamp, one of the few not connected to the electric timer. He took one look at the oriental rug and protested that he'd drip on it. Someone had brought the kid up right. It made me think, and after I fetched a dry towel I asked him if he wanted to call his folks. Or somebody. To tell them he was okay.

"I called from the police station," he said. "They won't worry." I wasn't sure if he was lying or not, but I like to start off believing my clients so I let it ride.

I pulled a spiral notebook out of the bottom left-hand drawer of the desk and headed the first page with the date, Jerry's name, and his address. I asked him for a phone number and he gave me one right off. Then he said I should probably have his parents' number, too.

"You don't live together?"

"Sure we do. I just gave you the line to my room."

I don't come from the kind of background where kids have their own phones. Paolina's housing project doesn't run to private lines for the kiddies.

"Okay," I said. "Tell me about Valerie."

I got her full name and address. Her phone, but Jerry

didn't know if the rest of the family shared it. Her mother's name was Mathilde. Jerry thought it was spelled with an "e" on the end, not an "a." Her father was Preston W., and he was a banker, or maybe an investment counselor. Probably had to become a banker with that name. "Preston W. Haslam" had the ring of old money and I thought I might have heard it around. On the other hand, it may just have had that generic banker chime. Valerie had a little sister, maybe five or six, and Jerry wasn't sure of her name, possibly Sherri. Something cute, with an "i" on the end.

"When did Valerie run away?" I asked.

"She didn't. She's not the type—"

"Yeah," I said. "When did she disappear?"

"I saw her, uh, Monday, the fourth. I don't think anybody's seen her since then. That's not right. I mean, it's not right, is it?"

"It seems odd," I said.

"Valerie's a great kid, really," Jerry said, as if I'd been about to cast aspersions her way. "I mean she hasn't been doing so hot at school lately, but she wouldn't run away because she flunked some stupid class."

"What school?" I asked.

"Oh," he said. "The Emerson."

If rumor was true, the boy could afford my rates. The Emerson School was supposedly the ritziest private academy in Massachusetts, a state that's no slouch in snob schools.

"What did she flunk?" I asked.

"Biology. And she was going to flunk drama, which is totally hard to do, but then I guess she turned in her stuff, so she was only really in trouble in biology. She could have gotten a tutor, or taken an incomplete."

"Were you looking for her tonight? In the Zone?"

He stared down at the rug, lifted the ice pack to his lip.

"Why did you think she'd run there?" I tried again.

"I said I didn't think she'd run away."

"Why were you looking for her there?"

"I had some other business. I don't know what I was thinking. I'm really tired." He was going to add that his mouth hurt, but I guess I wasn't old enough to rate the confidence. From the way he looked at me, I had the uneasy feeling that he still classed me as a girl he wanted to impress.

"Want to tell me what happened to your mouth?"

"I walked into a wall."

"Before or after you talked to the police?"

"Jesus," he said, "they're not gonna find Valerie. You know how many missing kids there are in Boston? A thousand. A thousand missing kids. And then this guy said I should talk to this Youth Assistance Unit. That sounded great, you know, until I figured out it's two cops. Two cops looking for a thousand kids. Shit. It's unbelievable. Totally."

"They get busy," I said.

"I asked about you. They said you used to be a cop."

"Yeah."

"Why'd you quit?"

"Why don't you tell me more about Valerie?" I said. "Her friends. Her habits."

"Geez," he said. "Really, I don't know where to start. There's so much shit that's not important to anybody. And I don't know where she's gone."

"Let me decide what's important, okay?"

Valerie was fourteen, almost fifteen, by Jerry's way of

counting. She was left-handed. She had one really close girlfriend, Elsie McLintock. She'd lived in the same house all her life. She broke her left arm when she was twelve, while ice-skating. She liked to wear knitted wool hats in the winter. Her favorite color was pink. She knitted Jerry a sweater once. She liked to knit and she liked to skate. She was a pretty decent skater.

I like ice-skating. It's the only exercise I can stand besides volleyball. I can skate forward and backward, but I can't do any of the loop-de-loop fancy stuff. Valerie could.

Valerie despised field hockey. She was a good dancer. She didn't cheat on tests, like most of the kids. She had a small scar on the inside of her left wrist. He didn't know how it had happened. It had always been there. Maybe it was a birthmark. There was lots of that kind of stuff. I asked him to describe her, and his hand reached for his wallet. When he realized his picture of Valerie was gone along with his money, his face got even paler, and I decided that sixteen or seventeen didn't matter. He was still a kid and he'd had a long day.

I got a blanket and a pillow out of the hall closet and told him he could sleep on the couch for a couple of hours. Plenty of time for the inquisition to continue after sunrise.

CHAPTER 5

There's a dress code for taxi drivers in this town. Shirts have to have collars, and no shorts are allowed, not even on the hottest August scorcher. Private investigators, on the other hand, can wing it. After two hours of blissfully undisturbed slumber, I went downstairs, attired in an electric blue sweater and black wool slacks.

The blanket was folded neatly on the couch, the pillow smoothed and piled on top of it. I called Jerry's name. Nothing. I checked to see if the bathroom was occupied. The client seemed to have flown the coop, which puzzled me because I have deadbolt locks on all the doors, so you need a key to leave as well as enter my dwelling.

Then I met Roz coming out of the kitchen.

Roz is always a delight to the eye. This morning her hair was the color of cranberries, the kind that slide out of the can in a log. She wore a fuschia T-shirt that almost met the hem of a thigh-high black denim skirt, black lace pantyhose with a run up the right leg, and green leather pointy-toed ankle boots. Roz is short and skinny, except for her breasts. With Roz, first you notice her hair, because it's generally an unnatural color, then you notice her eyes, because she wears killer makeup—fake eyelashes and glued-on sequins—and then you become aware of her breasts, because they're emphatically there and because she has the world's best T-shirt collection, bar none. This one featured a picture of Smokey, and said: DEFEND YOUR RIGHT TO ARM BEARS.

I'm fascinated by Roz's shoes. She wears one of those ridiculously small sizes, a five or something, so she can buy all these weird shoes nobody else wants. They have mounds of them in Filene's Basement, cheap. Today's ankle boots had incredibly skinny four-inch heels. She was perched so high on her toes that her feet looked like little hooves.

Well, not really. It's just shoe jealousy. Size eleven shoes, on the rare occasion you can find them, come in basic brown.

"He in there?" I asked, nodding toward the kitchen.

"Huh?" she replied, licking a sticky finger. Roz eats peanut butter for breakfast, straight from the jar. She has mastered the art of not looking after herself. She does all the cleaning, and she's figured out that if you don't make it dirty you don't have to clean it. Some days she can go entirely without forks, spoons, knives, plates, or glasses. I'm glad we keep separate food supplies, because when Roz's fingers are not stained with peanut butter they're usually covered with paint, turpentine, or developer fluid.

I admire Roz's basic laziness. Other people her age, which I put at around twenty, are out doing aerobics and eliminating toxins. They're improving their eating habits, getting in touch with their inner selves. Roz has a T-shirt that says "Live Hard, Die Young." McDonald's is her idea of a health food restaurant.

"I have a missing client," I said. "He spent the night on the couch."

"Oh," she said. "That was a client." Her tone let me know she thought he was my version of the Twin Brothers. Which was dumb because Jerry Toland, though attractive, would have been cradle-snatching for Roz, never mind me. And if I had stooped to cradle-snatching why the hell would the snatchee have been sleeping on the couch? "He had to leave," she continued. "I let him out. He's cute."

"Great," I said.

"Trouble?" she said.

"Somebody come for him?" I asked.

"Nope."

"Anybody waiting for him outside?"

"Nah."

"Terrific," I said flatly.

"He left you a note."

"Where?"

"I stuck it on the fridge."

That's one of our methods of communication. I probably would have noticed the note within the next three months. Roz is supposed to keep the refrigerator-door-bulletin-board organized, toss out year-old messages, expired supermarket coupons, stuff like that, but she rarely does.

This note was more like a scrap, a torn sheet of an address book that took some deciphering. It said, "Try Elsie first. Sorry to run. Thanks for everything." At least that's what Roz thought it said. Jerry had terrible handwriting.

Roz started humming a jingle from a TV commercial. She keeps the tube blaring while she paints, and it does strange things to her mind and her art. She seemed brisk and cheerful, like she'd slept nine hours instead of caterwauling most of the night. I needed to talk to her, to make a declaration about the bathroom and the Twin Brothers. I needed to say that while I didn't care with whom she slept, I didn't want her sleeping arrangements to taint her judgment concerning bathroom design.

"Carlotta," she said as if she could read my mind, "hey, you worried about the Brothers?"

"Right," I said.

"Relax, okay?"

"Why?"

"The bathroom's gonna knock you out. Shazam!"

"Roz, I want a bathroom the cat won't be embarrassed to pee in, okay? I don't want state of the art. I want your basic normal bathroom."

"But you said—"

"I said beige, not black. I said pink, not orange. Are they color-blind, or deaf, or what?"

"Carlotta, you gotta trust me," she said. She smiled

enigmatically and waltzed out the door. I could hear her heels tap up the stairs.

I felt like going back to bed and starting over. Instead I opened the fridge, found a carton of Tropicana, and poured a tumblerful. Orange juice clears my head.

Roz had deserted her copy of the *Herald*—I get the *Globe*—on the kitchen table, and sure enough, they had Mooney's story on page one, milking it for all it was worth. Reading between the lines, they seemed to be trying to link him to the other current police scandal, the one about collecting special-duty pay for not showing up at bars and sporting events. I could no more see Mooney taking cash for a job he hadn't done than I could see him roughing up somebody during an arrest, but I admit, the article made me think.

I wondered what shape Mooney's finances were in. I wondered if his mom had been sick, if he'd had any special expenses lately. Then I realized that all across New England people were doing likewise, looking for reasons for Mooney's fall from grace, even though the *Herald* was careful to use "alleged" in every other sentence. People who didn't even know Mooney were clucking over his downfall. That made me mad. I wondered if Mooney hid the papers from his mom.

I tossed the *Herald* in the trash and reread Jerry Toland's note. After a glass and a half of orange juice, I had the presence of mind to go into the living room, come back with my notebook, and leaf through the pages until I discovered the name "Elsie" in with last night's scribblings: Elsie McLintock, Valerie's best friend.

I reviewed my notes and was struck by how little

Jerry had actually revealed about Valerie. The girl existed in negatives. She wasn't prom queen or valedictorian or most talented. I'd had to lead him, prompt him, for a physical description. She had brown hair. Light or dark? I don't know. There's like, this gold color in it. Her eyes were, like, this gray, or maybe green. She stood barely shoulder high, which I made out to be five-foot-four, and maybe she was a little on the skinny side.

She was quiet, shy, but she liked her drama class. She didn't belong to any one group at school. You couldn't classify her as a prep or a nerd or a jockette. She didn't do drugs. Jerry was vehement about that. Maybe too vehement.

I'd hardly learned anything about Valerie's family. Damn that Jerry. The manner of his departure did not sit well with me.

Elsie McLintock had been noted as somebody who'd have a picture of Valerie. That would help, what with the weakness of Jerry's description.

I went to the cupboard and checked out the cereal boxes. I wasn't in the mood for Raisin Bran and the freshness date on the Corn Flakes was long past.

How do you describe people anyway? I could tell by his eyes, by his voice, that Jerry Toland cared about Valerie Haslam. How do you define the people you love? Paolina has brown hair, but "brown" says nothing about the shimmer and sway of it, the way a strand of it might curl against her cheek or tickle her nose. And if I tried to explain Paolina, I'd have to start with her laugh, a bubble of merriment that bursts when you least expect it. Paolina's laughter seems like a special reward, reserved for me.

Well, Paolina was in Colombia, to me as "missing" as Valerie Haslam.

I ate breakfast. A bagel, cream cheese, coffee with cream and sugar. On a plate. In a cup. With silverware and a napkin. I'm profligate that way.

"Start with Elsie." Not me. I started with the phone. I called local hospitals, jails, and finally the morgue. No Valerie Haslams. No unidentified teenage female Caucasians. I dialed the girl's house, because I figured her parents ought to know about the whole business. Maybe Valerie would answer and then I could rip up Jerry's IOU along with the standard contract form he'd insisted on signing, legal or not. I got an answering machine with a gruff male voice. I left my name and number.

The doorbell buzzed three times, the signal for Roz. I heard her flying down the steps, clattering in her tiny boots. She greeted the Twin Brothers with equal enthusiasm, as if she hadn't just spent most of the night with one of them.

It's cowardly, I know, but I decided to flee before the destruction began. It was way too early for Mooney's hooker to make an appearance in the Zone, so I decided to follow Jerry's advice and start with Elsie. Why not? Valerie's parents weren't home, and kids have to be in school, right?

On my way out the door the telephone rang. The stern voice on the other end identified herself as Mrs. Mooney, the lieutenant's mother. She wanted to know if I could drop by the apartment. Anytime would be good. Now would be preferable.

CHAPTER
6

Back when I was a cop, I used to drive by Mooney's place in my cruiser and imagine what it was like inside. Now I parked my Toyota down the block and stared up at the brick building. Aside from a fanlight over the front door, the architect hadn't gone in for many fancy touches. Four stories high, the dingy yellow brick square was peppered with rectangular windows. The three steps up to the door were plain concrete, flanked by two urns that should have held geraniums. The right-hand urn was broken, a section of lip still jagged. The left-hand one was whole, with a thin layer of dirt in the bottom.

The Mooney clan used to live in South Boston, an Irish stronghold renowned for stoning buses full of black kids. Mooney got tired of being labeled a bigot on the basis of his address and moved to the Hemenway Street apartment right after the cops nailed a ring of firebugs who were turning the Symphony Road area into a Beirut look-alike. His mom wanted him to come home to Southie when his father died, but Mooney's stubborn. He kept his apartment, so Mom sold the family homestead, and moved in with her only son.

I checked out the on-street parking, hoping to spot Mooney's battered Buick. Seven cars sported parking tickets.

Mooney doesn't talk much about his mother. What I know about her can be summed up in few words: cop's widow, cop's mother. I met her once at the station and got the strong impression she didn't care for female cops. Maybe that's why I summed her up as a member of the Ladies Auxiliary, defining her in terms of her husband and son. I never do that to women I like—or even to women I know.

I didn't know much about Mooney's mom. Not even her given name. To me she existed as a presence— stern, forbidding, righteously Catholic—and I wasn't sure if I'd picked the image up from Mooney or constructed it on my own.

Her sharp voice on the phone hadn't helped.

I patted my hair down before I rang the bell. The automatic gesture made me pause. I used to do it all the time, back when I was an insecure teenager. Now— well, if my hair's too wild, too bad. But the instinctive response made me wonder if I wanted to impress Mooney's mom. And why.

The minute I hit the bell, her voice came over the loudspeaker. She must have been waiting for me. Maybe she'd watched me approach from a curtained window. When I gave my name, she buzzed me in. The interior door was heavy wood, solid, with bars blocking a dusty window. The foyer smelled musty and the gray stair carpeting had seen long years of use.

I didn't have to search for 3B. The door was already open and Mrs. Mooney hovered in the doorway. I wouldn't have known her.

She wore a shapeless pink housedress that hung straight from her shoulders, covered by a worn beige cardigan. Her gray hair was full and lush, obviously a wig. The contrast between the glossy hair and the sunken face was too great. There was a hint of Mooney around her jaw. Heavy lines creased her brow and dragged her face down in discontented folds.

She favored me with a faint smile, but she'd lost none of her peremptory telephone manner.

"Come in," she said, and it wasn't an invitation but an order.

"How do you do," I said formally, "I'm Carlotta Carlyle."

"Peg Mooney," she said, extending a frail hand. "I remember you in uniform."

She closed the door after me, leaning on it heavily. Then she transferred her weight to the rubber grips of an aluminum walker.

"Please," she said briskly, "have a seat on the couch. It takes me a little while to set myself up in the chair. Would you like some lemonade?"

There was a glass on the coffee table with a little lace doily underneath, sheltering the wooden table from harm. Not that it had ever been a good piece of wood, but whatever care and polish could do for it they'd done.

The room was like that. The fabric on the green brocade sofa looked thin enough to shred, threadbare with careful cleaning. The smocked throw pillows were twenty years old if they were a day, their once-gold taffeta graying at the edges. Too much furniture had been stuffed in the small room, too many quaint little ornamental tables and footstools. Too many doilies and cushions and knickknacks. The effect was that of a larger room condensed. It made me claustrophobic and I wondered how Mooney stood it, Mooney who had a desk and a chair and a single picture in his office.

I was certain the furnishings dated from the Mooney childhood home, too worn to resell and too "good" to give away. Was Mooney's room different or had he let Mom do whatever she wanted with his apartment?

I tried to help Mrs. Mooney with the slow business of sitting down, but she nodded me away almost angrily. My grandmother used to do everything for herself too. Stubborn as six mules, my mom used to call her, with a hint of admiration.

I never met my mother's mother, though I was brought up on a steady diet of her Yiddish sayings. When my mother married outside the faith—a non-Jew, a Catholic—my strictly Orthodox grandmother refused to see her again. She mourned her daughter and chanted the traditional prayers for the dead. Over the passing years, she relented. She'd speak to my mother on the telephone, at first only on her birthday, later every Friday evening—early—before sundown and the *shabbas* made the use of machinery unthinkable. My mother always said that if my *bubbe* had lived even another month they'd have reconciled, and the two of us would have met.

Instead I went with my mother to help clean out *Bubbe's* apartment after her death. My photograph, an ornately framed enlargement of a snapshot Mom had sent her long ago, had pride of place on the living room wall. My grandmother had never acknowledged receiving it.

The musty smell I associated with age and stubbornness, sickness and death, clung to Mooney's place.

The *Herald* was on the coffee table, the story about Mooney face-up below the front-page fold. I wanted to hide it.

Peg Mooney saw my eyes take it in, and she stuck her chin out defiantly.

"You read that, I guess," she said, lowering herself into the chair. It was a slow process. She clutched the walker until she was maybe eight inches above the cushion, then let go and collapsed abruptly with a sigh.

I pretended to be fascinated by my glass of lemonade. It was good, fresh-squeezed and tart. I hoped Mooney had made it because I couldn't stand the thought of his mother going to all that work for me, squeezing lemons with her weak, clawed hands.

"My son doesn't know I called you," she began.

I waited, watching her.

"And I don't want him to know. There are things I don't want to know about in his life and things I don't want him to know about in mine. We live in each other's pockets but privacy is still important, I think."

I nodded my agreement, drank lemonade.

"I know you used to work for Joseph," she said.

It took me a minute to realize that Joseph was Mooney. I knew his name was Joe, but nobody ever used it.

"And since you used to be a policewoman, I assume you know people in the department still."

"I do," I said. Over her head on the far wall were framed photographs, like in my grandmother's flat, some black and white, some in older sepia tones. One must have been Mooney as a little boy. He wore a sailor suit and his face was fuller and softer, but essentially the same.

"All my friends on the force are retired," she said. "Well really, they were never my friends. They were Pat's friends, my husband's drinking buddies. The wives were tolerated, not like now . . . But I know it's all changed since the old days. The young cops aren't the same. College cops, my Pat used to call them, and he'd look down his nose at them, though he never made it out of high school. He was a fine policeman, my husband, seven citations for bravery, and shot once before the end. Gave his life to the department, just like my boy."

I settled in and drank lemonade. I'd been invited to listen to reminiscences. Well, I'd lived through worse. If it helped her forget her pain for a while I could certainly spare the time. Her voice softened when she talked about "her Pat" and I could catch the faintest hint of a brogue. I searched the wall for a photograph of a younger Mrs. Mooney. She was there in her wedding gown, smiling shyly, with no suffering in her eyes.

"Is there anything I can get you?" I asked her. "I could make you some coffee, or tea."

"No, thank you," she said, stiffening immediately

when I brought her back to the present. "But there's something you can do for me. You can explain how a man can give his whole life to the department and then have them all turn on him over nothing."

"I don't think I can explain that," I said.

"The *Herald* would never have printed garbage like that when my husband was alive. The police would never have broken ranks and talked about one of their own like that, and to a reporter."

"Your son must have explained what happened—"

"He doesn't talk about it. He pretends it didn't happen and he goes off every day somewhere like he had to go to work, only now I know he's not going to work. I thought maybe he came to you. . . ."

"No," I said.

"Are you Catholic?" she asked out of the blue.

"No," I said flatly.

"Ah," she murmured. "He wouldn't tell me that."

"Is it so important?" I asked.

"Yes," she said without batting an eye. "To me."

"Mrs. Mooney, what can I do for you?"

"My son thinks you're trustworthy."

"I think highly of your son," I said. "He's a fine policeman and a fine person."

She gestured to the wall of photos over her shoulder. "There's a picture of him here with his wife," she said. "Go take a look. Such a handsome couple they are."

I wanted to correct her. His ex-wife. But then, she probably didn't recognize their divorce. I got up and crossed the room.

It was an eight-by-ten studio portrait, and Mooney's wife was lovely, with a soft, smiling face. Petite. Blonde. High Slavic cheekbones. She clung to

Mooney's arm, and he wore a smile so carefree it was almost painful.

I turned my attention to another picture, one of a stern-faced man. "Is this your husband?" I asked.

"The one in uniform," she said. "That's Pat. Always in uniform. He was a beat cop till the day he died and proud of it."

I went back to the sofa and sat down gently to save the upholstery.

"Well, Miss Carlyle," she said, "if I still knew people in the department I wouldn't need you to . . ."

"To what?" I said when she faltered.

"Would you like more lemonade?" she asked. "It's no bother . . ."

"No, thank you," I said.

"Listen," she said, "if you really work as a private cop, I want to hire you to do a task for me. I'd do it myself, but I'm too lame and too slow."

"What task?"

"I have a little money put by. I can pay you for it."

"What task?" I repeated.

"In the old days, I wouldn't have needed to do this. The department used to take care of its own, you know?"

I waited, full of foreboding.

"I want you to talk to the policeman, the one who wrote up the report, and I want you to convince him that he saw a knife, that he made a mistake on the paperwork, you know?"

"Please," she went on when I said nothing. "It's not too late, just because of what the papers say. Things get lost at police stations. Maybe the knife was in the man's pocket and they found it later at the hospital, but one of the orderlies stole it or something. There are ways to manage it with no one getting hurt.''

''You don't think there was a knife, do you?'' I said gently.

''I don't care,'' she replied.

''You think your son beat that guy up and lied about it?''

''Listen to me, girl,'' she said angrily. ''It doesn't matter to me whether there was a knife or a gun or a machete or a machine gun. My boy is a good cop, like his father was.''

''Times have changed,'' I said.

''And not for the better.''

''Did his father beat people up?'' I shouldn't have challenged her, but I couldn't help it. There was a gleam in her eye and she answered me like she'd been waiting for a fight and I was the selected opponent.

''People that needed beating, yes, and he wasn't ashamed of it. None of this modern 'be kind to the scum of the earth' garbage, and let them come back and shoot you tomorrow. My husband knew which side he was on.''

''That must have been a comfort to him.''

''It was,'' she said. ''Oh, it was.''

''So you want me to bribe a police officer,'' I said quietly. I finished the last drop of lemonade and put the glass back on the table, in the exact center of the crocheted doily. ''You know your son would hate it.''

''He wouldn't know,'' she said. ''That's part of your job. I want it handled tactfully. I can pay you a hundred dollars, and for the officer another hundred.''

"No," I said. "I'm sorry. I can't."

"Then maybe you'll do it because you care what happens to Joseph. This is eating him up, killing him."

"Mrs. Mooney, believe me, there's no way to handle this tactfully, no way to handle it at all. I'm not going to take the job, and I won't say anything about it to your son. And, please—promise me—don't try it yourself. You'll just make things worse for him."

"Worse for him," she said. "Worse for him? And how do you think things could get worse for him?"

I didn't say anything.

"Go on," she said. "Get out."

I thanked her for the lemonade, but she pretended not to hear me, sitting in stony silence like a carved figure of herself. I said good-bye, and almost ran down the steps to the front door. I needed to get the taste of that lemonade out of my mouth, the sick smell of the apartment out of my nostrils.

I drove out to the Emerson School much too fast. The speedometer kept creeping up—ten, twenty, twenty-five miles over the Route 2 limit. I was lucky I didn't get stopped by a cop.

CHAPTER
7

Jerry had vowed money was no problem, but I don't think I believed him until I strolled onto the freshly mown lawn of the Emerson. That's what the place is called. They just drop the "School" part, because anybody who is anybody knows that the Emerson is a prep school, a toney private high school.

If this was a high school, what I went to in Detroit was cruel and unusual punishment.

It wasn't just the putting-green grass. Well-pruned bushes, stately firs, and classy red brick buildings contributed to the mini-Harvard effect. But instead of the surrounding bustle of Harvard Square, the Emerson was ringed by acres of landscaped countryside. The admissions committee probably interviewed the squirrels, and only took the ones that would eat out of your hand.

No bell rang, but the quadrangle suddenly flooded with students. The girls all seemed to be wearing skirts—not uniform kilts or anything—but skirts of differing colors and lengths. They giggled, a reassuringly teenaged noise. The boys wore sports jackets with open-collared white shirts.

Must be a dress code, I said to myself. I couldn't believe these kids had deliberately chosen to look like junior execs at IBM. A few signaled their individuality with semi-punk hairdos. Mild by Roz's standards, undoubtedly revolutionary at the Emerson.

They carried books. We did that in Detroit. It gave me a basis for comparison. This probably was a school.

I should have reported directly to the office. That's what the exquisitely lettered notice on the stone front gate said: VISITORS REPORT DIRECTLY TO OFFICE. I fully intended to until I saw that sign. Once inside a high school, hospital, jail—anyplace they keep you prisoner—I turn ornery. I do whatever they tell you not to do. I'm a truant at heart.

I sought camouflage. No way was I going to meld with the student body. I could maybe pull off a high school student imitation at a normal high school, wearing jeans and a T-shirt, but here, in the midst of all this teenage formality, my interviewing-the-client slacks and sweater looked wrong. I assumed a mask of authority. Maybe I could play teacher.

There are things I could teach these kids, believe me. Starting with city smarts. Also self-defense, blues guitar, and volleyball.

I scouted around, entering a couple of the red brick buildings unchallenged. One of them had a framed diagram of the campus on a pale gray wall. Imagine, a campus. My high school was a city square block—eight floors, no elevators—and so overcrowded that classes were held on the roof as well as in the park across the street. Which was worse, no one was sure. Park classes meant the possibility of getting mugged; students on the roof were fair game for stray bullets from the ROTC rifle range.

The Emerson seemed to have plenty of space. Space for a foreign language lab, a student lounge, a cafeteria, a computer center, a school store, a little theater, and stables. Yes, riding stables.

The only horses I saw in Detroit were mounted patrol, brought in to quell riots.

I decided to wander, to soak up the privileged atmosphere Valerie had abandoned. Outside, the grounds were deserted. Everybody was in class, pulled by an invisible magnet. The air smelled like fresh-mown grass. The sun glistened. A thin stoop-shouldered man repaired a goal net on the soccer field.

I was debating a belated trip to the office when I remembered that all high school kids have to take gym. Including Elsie McLintock. In my guise as freelance volleyball instructor, keeping the diagram of the school in my head, I found the right building and entered inconspicuously through huge double doors.

The gym was enormous, but I expected no less from the Emerson. To my delight, a ragged volleyball game was in progress. I sat in the stands, exhausted by all the elegance, welcoming the familiar smell of sneakers and sweat socks.

I knew Elsie McLintock's name. I didn't know what she looked like or even what class she was in. I assumed she was a freshman because Valerie was a freshman, and years mean so much when you've experienced so few.

A cheer came from the court. One game decided and handslapping all around. Two girls on the winning team—one short, one tall—could play. They roamed the court, poaching at will. Their teammates played like they were scared to sweat.

I play killer volleyball three mornings a week at my local Cambridge YWCA. It's terrific exercise and lacks the pointlessness of, say, stationary bicycling. Somebody gets to win; somebody gets to lose. I love it. I'm an outside hitter—a spiker—but I can play middle blocker if I have to.

One of the girls who didn't mind sweat came out winded, and a replacement ran in for her. She sat two rows in front of me.

"Good game," I said, moving down beside her.

"Thanks." She was breathing hard.

"Tired?"

"I had mono, and now I can't move. It's like taking forever to get back."

Forever at her age was probably two weeks.

I said, "Do you know Elsie McLintock?" I figured I might as well try. It was a small school—in enrollment, not area.

"Elsie?"

"Yeah. McLintock. She's a freshman."

"I think I've heard the name."

"You know when she has gym?"

"Nah." She was watching the game. She had one of

those classic WASP profiles with the slightly turned-up nose that makes you look snotty even if you aren't. She brushed her thick blonde hair back off her forehead. I took advantage of the fact that well-bred girls with glossy manes rarely tell an adult to butt out.

"You know where I could find her?"

"Ms. Sutton has the schedule cards," she said, watching the game intently.

"Ms. Sutton?"

"Laura, the one with the French braids."

One of the girls who played hard and well was really the teacher.

"Thanks," I said.

A small office opened off the right-hand side of a basketball court. I figured Ms. Sutton was not going to make a sudden appearance because the game was tight and her team needed her. She was a well-organized teacher, with four index card files on her desk, neatly marked by class. I snitched Elsie's card from the freshman file, and I'm sorry for any inconvenience that may have caused Ms. Sutton. I wish she played on my team at the Y. She was short, even for a setter, but spunky. She made a couple of fairly impossible digs, and even spiked a few, which is tough for a shorty.

I checked my wristwatch. In half an hour Elsie McLintock would pass from English block to Social Studies block. That gave me thirty minutes to find out whether a block was a building or a unit of time, and what Elsie looked like.

The block business was easy. I went back to the building with the diagram and found English block listed in the legend at the bottom of the map. Identifying Elsie was trickier. They didn't have student photos posted. It looked pretty futile until I realized every classroom had a phone.

I located Elsie's English class, room 121, with little trouble. All English classes were in the English block, all language classes were in the Language block, all math classes were in another red brick house and so on. I found an empty room across the hall, took the receiver off the hook, and punched 121, wondering who I'd reach. Sometimes internal phone systems have a code. You know, you have to dial nine first or something. The buzz in Elsie's classroom was so loud it startled me.

Elsie's teacher, a chubby, balding man, crossed the room and I ducked behind the door.

"Sorry to interrupt," I said quickly. "Elsie McLintock to the office, please."

"Sarah?" the deep voice said.

I made a monosyllabic neutral response. It's so easy to lie on the phone.

"I really can't have these interruptions."

"I'm sorry," I said very sincerely. "Please send her right away. It's urgent."

As the girl left the room I followed her.

She was small. Tidy. Light brown hair fell in a well-cut curve to her shoulders. She wore a gray denim knee-length skirt and a pastel flower-patterned shirt. Two gold bracelets clinked on her wrist.

"Elsie," I called.

She turned. At least I'd gotten the right one.

"You don't need to go to the office."

"But Mr. Chesney said— Who are you?"

"Jerry Toland hired me to find Valerie."

"Humph," she said, or something like it.

"Can we go someplace and talk?" I asked.

"I'll be late for American Studies."

"Do you know where Valerie is?"

"No."

"Do you care?"

She gave me a look. "Well, of course. She's my friend."

"Then we need to talk."

"There's the lounge," she said reluctantly.

"Fine," I said.

She led the way to this immense multileveled cushioned room, done in soothing blues. I didn't see why any of the kids went to class when they could snooze on deep blue velvet couches. We sat on one of them. I ran my hand over the smooth plush.

"What did you say your name was?" Elsie's folks must have told her not to talk to strangers. I passed over one of my business cards. They seem to have a calming effect, although for eighteen bucks you can get three hundred printed to say you're the President.

The girl gave me the once over and I felt like she was estimating the cost of my clothes. "Why did Jerry go to you? I mean, did he look in the Yellow Pages?"

I kept my temper in check. "Well, I suppose he's worried about Valerie."

"I'll bet."

"Is that supposed to be sarcastic?"

She didn't reply.

"Did Valerie say anything to you about going away?" I asked. "Running away?"

She shook her head no. The brown hair bounced. She used too much makeup, too pale a foundation. Dark liner encircled her narrow eyes, and her lips were pale purple. If I had to choose a word to sum her up, "sullen" would be a leading contender.

"Did you get the feeling Valerie was unhappy?" I said.

"In this dump? You kidding?"

"This is a dump?"

"School is awful, you know."

With that off her chest, she pulled out a pack of Virginia Slims and lit up. I resisted the impulse to slap her hand. I'm an ex-smoker myself—started before her age—but it startles me when I see kids light up. I mean, these days they know what they're doing to their lungs. They can read it right on the box.

"Want one?" she said.

"No thanks," I said mildly, refraining from pointing out the Surgeon General's warning and trying not to gulp down the second-hand smoke too eagerly. "Are Valerie's folks worried about her?"

"Probably frantic," she said as if she were enjoying the idea. "That is, if they even know."

She was so unconcerned I wanted to shake her.

"Wait a minute," I said. "Maybe I'm not understanding something. Does Valerie live here? Board here?"

"She lives at home. I board."

"So Valerie's parents would notice if she didn't turn up for the night, right?"

"She's not a child, Ms., uh, Carlyle. They'd probably assume she was staying with somebody here."

"With you?"

"Maybe. But she isn't with me."

"Did you call her parents to ask if she's sick or something?"

"Look, Valerie's not dumb. She's not going to hop in a car with some rapist, you know. She's got judgment. She's been to New York."

I didn't see where the last two statements jibed.

"You know," Elsie said in a further attempt to convince me, "she's almost fifteen. She can quit school next year, and they can't do a damn thing about it." She made "fifteen" sound like "forty-five."

"What about you?" I asked.

"What do you mean?"

"Why do you think she ran away?"

She stared at the top textbook in her pile of three— *Analytic Chemistry*. "I can't say."

"Can't or won't?"

"Can't," she said.

"When was the last time you saw her?"

"I didn't write it down," she said.

"Think," I said.

"I'm gonna be late," she said.

"Right," I said.

"Monday, and then she called me Monday night."

"From home?"

"I guess."

"Was she upset?"

"No."

"Anything unusual about the conversation?"

"No." She looked pointedly at her wristwatch, and said, "I'm going to get a detention."

"Is there somebody else I should talk to, another friend?"

"I'm Valerie's best friend. Nobody else would tell you anything."

"A teacher?"

She gave a deep sigh, probably at the impossibility of getting rid of me. "You could talk to Geoff, I guess."

"And Geoff is . . ."

"A teacher. We call a lot of the teachers by their first names. It encourages closeness."

Bullshit, I almost said.

"Where can I find this Geoff?" I asked.

"Drama block. On stage or in his office." She took a long drag on her cigarette and failed to look sophisticated. "He's dynamite," she added.

"Great," I said, deadpan. "Thanks so much for your help."

She ignored my tone and started to get up. I stopped her with, "Jerry said you'd have a picture of Valerie."

She pulled a gray leather shoulder bag onto her lap by its strap, took out a wallet, flipped through a bunch of credit cards, yes, credit cards—MasterCard, Visa, Gold American Express—until she found the right plastic sleeve. She pulled out a school photo—formal, airbrushed, perfect.

"You have to give this back," she said.

Valerie had a solemn smile that didn't get as far as her eyes. Her hair was smooth and fine, close to her skull, cut blunt at the chin. Her face was rounder than a perfect oval, her chin small and pointed. Her eyes were almond-shaped under light brows. Her nose was small, like the nose of a small child that hasn't yet taken on its adult shape. Her eyes were hazel, her blouse collar pale blue, her skin clear. I didn't think I'd seen a kid with acne anywhere on the school grounds. I wondered if they got expelled.

I flipped it over. On the back, in childish looping handwriting, it said:

Elsie

Remember: moles = grams over liters, Renaud's algebra factory, Fridays, EJB, Class notes, Flats and flatties, In your face, GR.

Love ya,
Valerie

"Love ya." Like Paolina closes her letters.

"Does she always call herself Valerie, never Val?" I asked.

"She despises Val."

Paolina hates nicknames, too. They tried to call her Paula at school last year, told her it was more "American." She got in a fight over it.

"Who's EJB?" I said.

"That's just junk. He's this guy I used to date. A jerk."

"Valerie date anybody?"

"Why don't you ask Jerry Toland about that? Ask Jerry why she left, okay?"

"What do you mean?"

"Just ask him," she said.

And then she walked away, swaying her hips, and trying so damn hard to look old.

CHAPTER
8

Locating Elsie used up my morning's share of luck. Even with detailed directions to the drama teacher's office, I couldn't find Geoff. He had split for the day, chaperoning a field trip, according to some future-stockbroker-of-America. I wondered where the students could have gone, what they might have wanted that wasn't provided on campus. Maybe they went to the city and watched poor people.

Geoff, whose brass name plate identified him as Mr. Geoffrey L. Reardon, left his office unlocked, probably to let his students know he had a deep and abiding trust in them. I peered casually down the hall, left and right.

Nobody. So I stepped inside and shut the door. Then I yanked down the shade on the single window and flicked on the desk lamp.

The office sported a braided rug, two chairs—one a comfortable-looking leather swivel, one a ladderbacked job—and an old oak desk. Nothing fancy, just what the Emerson had ordered back in seventeen-whatever when they'd opened, well-polished and gleaming. The desk faced the window. A wood-framed Degas ballerina print tilted on the wall near the door. Two framed diplomas hung nearby. Oberlin and NYU.

I don't display my diploma. UMass–Boston did well by me, but face it, it's not a classy school.

A low three-tiered bookshelf ran along one wall. The bottom two shelves were full of thin, brightly colored play scripts. The top shelf held mementos. A tarnished trophy with a golfing figure on top and Reardon's name at the base sat next to a squat Paul Revere bowl engraved with initials that didn't mean a thing to me. Two scrapbooks labeled "Drama Club" and filled with pictures of students in productions Reardon must have directed were propped open like kid's picture books, wreaking havoc on their spines. I flipped through them, hoping to find a picture of Valerie, one with some expression in her eyes, some indication of delight or despair or anxiety.

Reardon's productions seemed to involve a lot of teenage girls wearing bodysuits. I didn't see a shot of Valerie, but faces weren't the main focus of the photos.

Reardon's desktop was clear except for a split-leaf philodendron that needed watering, a telephone, and a thick manuscript clipped together with a long complicated metal arrangement along the left-hand margin.

The top sheet said: *"Wanderlust*, by Geoffrey L. Reardon."* The "L" had been scratched out, then added again. An arrow indicated that he was considering a change to "L. Geoffrey Reardon." The manuscript's corners were dog-eared, as if it had been read by more than a few people. Somebody had penciled comments. I read a page. It was a play. "Cecilia" and "David" seemed to be headed for divorce court.

CECILIA: You liar. You never called last night.
DAVID: You weren't home.

I read some more. It sounded like the stuff my ex and I used to sling back and forth. Expletives deleted.

I opened the top desk drawer and rifled Reardon's possessions, hoping for, say, a letter from Valerie with a return address. I didn't find one. I found her name in his rankbook, except I suppose you can't call it a rankbook when none of the students are ranked. There were check marks by each of the twelve names in Valerie's class, rows of check marks. At first I thought it was just an attendance book, but there were numbered assignments, all checked off. Whether one student was better than the next was something "L. Geoffrey" kept to himself. I wondered if the kids knew who did good work without the As and Fs to set them straight.

A studio portrait of a beautiful young man was face down in the lower left drawer. Signed from Stuart, with love. Maybe one of Geoff's students had become a Hollywood hunk. Maybe not. A famous student deserved a spot on the memento shelf. Maybe this was personal.

There was a pile of notebooks in the drawer, student work by the scrawls. I picked one up and glanced through the dated entries. The handwriting was enough to give you a headache.

The lower right-hand drawer was locked.

Locks are one of those small motor-skill things I do well, like guitar picking. Back when I was a cop, this felon taught me all about locks, even treated me to a set of picklocks before I busted him.

Reardon's desk lock wasn't much of a challenge, but it got the old adrenaline racing just because I knew I wasn't supposed to crack it. I felt a shiver up my spine when the lock clicked, and I breathed faster while I shoved my picks back in my shoulder bag and eased the drawer open.

A half-empty bottle of Wild Turkey and two smeared glasses glared at me. Some find.

I left my card on the desk with a message to call. Then I used the phone to try Valerie's parents again.

A soft-voiced woman answered and agreed when I addressed her as Mrs. Haslam. I started to explain who I was. She interrupted.

"Oh, yes, I know. I mean, Jerry told me about you. Miss—what's your name now? I know I had it here someplace. I wrote it on a scrap of paper. Never mind. He's such a good boy, Jerry that is. Did you know he was Valerie's best friend? Her best boyfriend, I should say; she has girlfriends, too. Not really a boyfriend, more a boy and a friend, you know. She's still so young . . .''

"Mrs. Haslam, Jerry got in touch with me because of your daughter's disappearance—''

"Yes, that's what he said. Such a dear boy. Did you see what happened to his mouth? I hope there won't be a scar or anything permanent or disfiguring or—''

It was my turn to interrupt. At first she went right on, blathering away about the cut on Jerry's lip, but I over-rode her through sheer volume and determination. "Is your daughter at home, Mrs. Haslam? Do you know where she is?"

"Well, I have two daughters, but of course you mean Valerie, don't you? Uh. Excuse me. Can you hang on just a minute? Thank you. I just want to turn the TV down. And I think I left something on the stove."

Turning the TV down and checking the stove took so long I thought we'd been disconnected. Just when I'd decided to hang up and call back, I heard her breathing into the phone.

"Oprah Winfrey's doing such an interesting show on teenagers," she said. "Teenage rebellion, you know. It seems like they all do it, but I don't know about Jerry—"

"Mrs. Haslam," I said loudly, "I want to talk to you about your daughter, Valerie. If you have time, I could come over now. I'm in Lincoln already, so I could be there in ten minutes."

"Oh, no," she said. "I don't think you'd better. I've been sick. A fever. I think it's catching. Fevers are usually catching, you know, and I wouldn't want you to—"

"Can you just confirm that Valerie is missing, Mrs. Haslam?"

"Well, it's not so easy," she said petulantly. "Valerie sometimes spends the night with a girlfriend. They're so independent at that age. Rebellion, like Oprah says. I don't want to make a fuss if all the girls do it, you know. Valerie would hate for me to make a fuss. And Preston, that's my husband, he's always saying I make scenes."

I felt like I was dropping down the rabbit hole in Alice-in-Wonderland. Unless Jerry Toland was fond of tall tales I was speaking to the mother of a missing four-teen-year-old girl who'd been gone a week. I had a strong suspicion the TV was still blaring, commandeering what little concentration Mathilde Haslam possessed.

"Is your husband at home?" I asked in desperation.

"Oh, no, dear," she said. "Preston wouldn't be home in the afternoon. He works, you know."

"Do you have a number where I can reach him?"

"You can't reach him today. He won't be in till late tonight. But I can have him call you as soon as he gets in."

"That would be fine," I said, speaking slowly. "Can you tell me the names of girls Valerie might be staying with? Her friends besides Elsie McLintock?"

"Oh, I'll call them," she said eagerly. "I should have done that before, shouldn't I? I'll call them and see if Valerie's there. Elsie's a sweet girl, isn't she? Like I told Jerry, I'm sure this is just some misunderstanding. I'm certain there's no need for everybody to get alarmed. Really, if you'll excuse me, I think I ought to lie down. My head is pounding so badly. The fever, you know—"

"Let me give you my phone number," I said quickly. "If you hear from Valerie I'd like to know. And have your husband call me."

Maybe he could hang on to a coherent thought.

I had to repeat my phone number three times. When I asked her if she'd written it down, she admitted she didn't have paper or pencil, and then took about ten minutes to locate them. I waited, shaking my head and tapping my fingers on Reardon's desk. She came back chattering about whatever was on the stove, her voice sounding even softer, with a blurry quality in spite of overly careful pronunciation. I wondered if her trip to the kitchen had included a stop for a drink.

This time I got her to repeat my number back to me. I spelled out my name twice. I think she got it.

"Don't worry," she told me before hanging up. "I'm sure everything's just fine."

I wasn't.

I switched off Geoff's desk lamp. As an afterthought I shifted the manuscript, ran my hand under the blotter, and found the key to his desk drawer, which made me feel dumb. I used it to lock up.

I was tempted to drop by the Emerson's office to check out the tuition rates. I wondered what it would cost to send Paolina. But on the way I looked around at the little ladies and gents marching to class with their designer labels and ninety-buck sneakers and carefully coiffed hair. There wasn't a Hispanic visible. I thought maybe Paolina would do better in Cambridge. Her school is tough, but so is she.

I headed back to Boston in a cold, gray drizzle that slicked the pavement. Despite the weather, the city looked great from far away. There's a place on Route 2 where you can see all the downtown skyscrapers. You crest a hill in Arlington and there it sits: a toy model of Boston. Usually it's in color, but today it looked like a black-and-white photograph, gun-metal building blocks stacked against a pale gray sky.

Closer up, the streets looked dirty. Dead leaves and brown snow clogged the gutters.

I went home, fed the bird, and fixed myself a toasted ham-and-cheese on rye. I turned on the radio and sat at the kitchen table to eat and deal with the mail. On WERS, Rory Block sang:

"Can't tell my future, Lord, I can't tell my past."

T.C. gets most of my mail since he's the one listed in the phone book. Today he got two begging letters from Presidential candidates, one Republican, one Democrat. I don't know how the Republicans got his name. He also received an urgent personal message from Ed McMahon.

I got an envelope with Mooney's address on the back flap, scrawled in his handwriting, thank God, so it wasn't from his mother. Inside was a check for two hundred bucks, marked "retainer" in that little space they leave for memos. I was going to rip it up, but then I decided it would be much more satisfactory to hand it back to him—once I'd found his hooker.

CHAPTER
9

I fumbled in the depths of my shoulder bag, locating seven lipsticks and a fistful of ballpoint pens before grabbing the right cylinder. I don't carry a full-sized flashlight—my purse weighs a ton already—but it's not some dinky toy that can barely light up a keyhole either.

I focused it on Valerie Haslam's photo, propped on the dashboard of the cab, and memorized her flawless skin, tiny nose, deep-set eyes. If I concentrated hard enough I could almost forget about impending frostbite.

Squirming lower in the front seat, I bent my left leg

and stuck my sneakered foot high on the dash. It wasn't comfy, but it was different. I checked to make sure my flannel shirt was buttoned to the chin and my down vest zipped all the way up. I wiggled my toes. I wasn't sure the baby one on the right foot was moving.

The good news: I nabbed one of Gloria's best cabs. When I flicked on the engine, warm air poured out of the heating vents.

The bad news: I waited two hours for the cab, so it was well past one in the morning with no sight or sound of Janine, the hooker, or Valerie, the runaway.

Mrs. Haslam hadn't called me off, so I assumed the girl was still missing. On the other hand, Mr. Haslam hadn't given me a buzz either. Probably Mrs. H. had tossed my phone number in the wastebasket as soon as I'd hung up.

I was parked near the same Combat Zone alley, my home away from home. Gangs of tough young Orientals patrolled the street corners, speaking words I couldn't understand. White-clad Danish sailors passed by—boyish, cold, and eager. One pounded on the hood of my cab. The sudden noise startled me, but he was just making a point to two gents sharing a bottle in a brown paper bag. Over on Washington Street, cars honked and gunned their motors. A saxophone player practiced the same mistakes, over and over. I didn't know the song.

I hadn't really minded waiting for the cab. Leroy, Gloria's baby brother, had been visiting. Gloria has these three brothers, each bigger and meaner than the last, all protective as hell of their sister. Leroy's my favorite. The youngest and smallest, rumor says he got kicked out of the NFL for biting some guy's ear off.

Leroy blows a mean blues harmonica, and Gloria owns an old guitar she never plays—an Epiphone that won't stay in tune more than a minute at a time. So Leroy and I left Gloria to juggle the phones, adjourned to her high-tech room-and-bath behind the garage, and jammed till my fingers bled. The action on that Epiphone is brutal.

I took off my gloves and explored the tips of my left-hand fingers with my thumb. My calluses aren't what they used to be.

I half hoped Sam Gianelli would drop by the garage. He hadn't, which was probably a good thing. I have mixed—very mixed—feelings about Sam.

Sam Gianelli owns half of Green & White Cab. We have history—the ancient kind from before I got married, back when I was just a kid hacking part time, and dumb enough to sleep with the boss.

We tried again six months ago. It didn't work out. For a lot of reasons.

That old Willie Brown blues ran through my mind again:

Can't tell my future, Lord, I can't tell my past.

Maybe the line was really "Can't tell my future, Lord, *if* I can't tell my past." I'd have to see if I could find it on a record. It's hard to understand the lyrics on some of those old-time recordings.

Sam is six-three and well-built, with a bony face and a stubborn jaw. My spine aches when he walks into a room.

If I'm physically attracted to a guy, if I breathe a little faster when he's near, it's practically a disaster warning. When that red flag goes up, I know I ought to run, not walk, to the nearest exit. Reverse chemistry, I call it. Whatever it is, I've got it with Sam.

He's the absentee partner in G&W. Gloria's the other half, and a more unlikely partner for gorgeous Sam Gianelli you'd need to scour the city to find. Gloria is a self-proclaimed "three-fer" who swears she's going to run for City Council some day and get elected so all the white males can say they've got a black, a woman, and a handicapped person on the job.

She'd get the overweight vote, too.

Gloria is not overweight through any metabolic trick. She's fat because she eats nonstop, junkfood only. She's the world Tootsie Roll–eating champion, and she's gaining on the record for most Hostess Cup-cakes consumed in a single day. Why she seems as cheerful as she does is a mystery to me. If I'd been para-lyzed from the waist down in a car crash at nineteen, I'd be damn bitter. Maybe Gloria was too, for a while, but now you can't even think about self-pity and Gloria at the same time. Maybe she takes it out in eating. I don't know.

Gloria is the queen bee of G&W. She rules the roost, which fronts on the less-than-scenic Mass. Pike in Allston, nestled in the middle of a row of cut-rate auto-glass replacement shops and used rug stores.

G&W's heartbeat issues from an ugly rectangular cell whose most attractive item of decor is a pegboard dan-gling with keys. It makes Geoff Reardon's office at the Emerson look like a *Better Homes and Gardens* spread. The floor is wavy linoleum, curled at one edge. The walls are army-surplus-green cinder block. A calendar, the gift of some defunct insurance company, livens up one wall. The matchstick blinds are broken. The file cabinets are gray and dented. Light is provided by unshaded hanging bulbs.

I don't go to Green & White for the atmosphere. I go to work, or I go to visit Gloria.

She has the world's most spectacular voice—mellow, rich, and deep, like a gospel singer's. I didn't meet her until long after I'd heard her belt our names and addresses over my cab radio. Green & White gets a lot of business from men who just want to hear that voice say she'll pick 'em up in five minutes.

A light flickered on in the building I was watching. I counted windows. It was one apartment over from Renney the pimp's place. No luck.

After Leroy had to leave for his club bouncer job, I flopped in Gloria's orange plastic guest chair, after checking it for roaches. I always catch little streaks of movement in that place. Small mice or big roaches, I'm not sure which. They banquet on the crumbs from Gloria's Twinkies.

"What do you hear, Glory?" I'd asked.

"Nothing," she'd said, feeling real conversational. She took a couple calls, moving cabs around the city. She can do five things at once, punch buttons on the phone console, relay addresses, play solitaire, eat Milky Ways. I spent some time admiring her outfit, which looked like a purple pup tent, to tell the truth.

"You working?" she'd asked after awhile.

"Two cases," I'd replied.

"Who-ee," she'd said. "Money pourin' in."

"Yeah, I'm gonna have to hire a Brink's truck." I didn't feel like telling her one of my clients was under age and the other was a freebie.

"You seein' that cop?" she'd asked.

"Mooney?" I'd answered cautiously. "Sometimes. Why?"

"You and he, uh, you dating or what?"

Dating is such a quaint word. "Nope," I'd said. I think Gloria likes to keep tabs on my love life, because of Sam. Maybe she reports to him.

"I hear he's gonna testify."

"Testify?" I'd repeated.

"At those hearings. You know," she'd said.

"What hearings?"

"Cops earning overtime for no-shows. Goosin' the bars that aren't connected. Givin' zero protection and takin' big bucks."

My stomach had contracted. If Mooney was going to testify, he must be involved.

The light in the flat next to Renney's died. I put my gloves back on and sat on my hands to warm them up.

My dad was a cop. Even now, hours after leaving Gloria, my stomach felt the way it used to when he and Mom had one of their roaring fights, way back before the divorce, when I was too small to remember much. I recalled one of their fighting words: "pad." "Pad," "on the pad," and its variations were unerring advance signals of pitched battles with pots and jars and ugly words hurtling through the air. I'd sit on the porch with my hands over my ears till the storm passed. I didn't find out what the words meant for years.

By then my dad was dead. I couldn't ask him.

A red Chevy Camaro, the car most likely to be ticketed by a cop or boosted by a thief, passed within inches of my fender, flying low, and brought me back to the present. It left a contrail of blaring acid rock.

I consulted Valerie's expressionless eyes. Was that her kind of music?

Fourteen and a half years old. I tried to remember fourteen, more than half a life ago. The quality of time had been so different. Everything, every single tiny want or need, had been urgent, immediate, absolutely wonderful, devastatingly awful. What would have made the fourteen-year-old me run from the Emerson School?

My mind balked. I couldn't picture myself there. What would make a kid from the suburbs run to the Zone? Had she run here? If not, why the hell had Jerry Toland followed? Why hadn't he reported his stolen wallet? Maybe he'd given it to Valerie. Maybe she'd lifted it while they argued.

I shifted position and started the engine, grateful for the rush of hot air. I decided to switch focus, forget Renney's place for the night, search for Valerie instead of Janine. Every cop in the city was probably keeping an eye out for bleached-blonde prostitutes, trying to get Mooney off the hook. As far as I knew, I was the only one looking for Valerie.

Maybe, said a small voice in my mind, if I keep a watchful eye on Valerie, someone will do the same for Paolina. I don't believe things balance out that way, but I figured it couldn't hurt.

I cruised the boundaries of the Zone, then criss-crossed the neon streets. I wondered how long it would take before the adult entertainment zone disappeared for good, what with Chinatown gaining on one side and New England Medical Center nibbling the other flank.

As soon as I stopped looking for Janine, I saw her.

She was moving toward a car. A man was with her. I couldn't see his face. He had an arm around her shoulder, squeezing hard. Hell, I couldn't see Janine that well, either. It just looked like her, from the staggering high-heeled walk to the tilt of her blonde head.

They got into a gray Chevy Caprice sedan, a driver already behind the wheel. The guy held the passenger door and waited while Janine scooted to the middle of the front seat. Then he shoved in beside her. He was heavyset, dark.

I was following the car before I remembered I was going to find Valerie first.

CHAPTER
10

The Chevy squealed away from the curb. In the front seat, Janine's frizzy blonde hair was sandwiched between a ducktail and a conservative banker-cut. The driver had narrow shoulders compared to the burly guy on the passenger side. I figured we were off for a quick romp to a nearby hotel.

We followed Washington Street to the turnpike access road, but instead of getting on the ramp to the Pike, the Caprice zigzagged onto Columbus Avenue and I started to worry.

Now I like tail jobs, but one-on-ones are tough. Darkness gave me the advantage. Taillights are individualistic. The Caprice had two rectangular panels, each made up of six red glass plates, three on top and three below. They worked in tandem, two plates to a set. The outside pairs blinked as turn signals. The inside and outside pairs of each set lit up when the driver hit the brakes. Either the left turn signal was broken or the man behind the wheel didn't believe in signaling lefts.

Most headlights look the same. With my rooflights off, I was just another set of round eyes in his rearview mirror. I kept well back, two hundred, three hundred yards.

When I drive I like music. Gloria's cabs, even the new ones, have dime-store radios, so I carry a mini-boombox that fits nicely on the passenger seat. I punched on my local blues station, came in on the tail end of an old Bonnie Raitt cut, and sang along, cruising easily behind the Chevy. I even cracked the front window, hoping for a breath of spring.

Columbus Avenue is not the place to smell spring. It's a place to lock your doors. I'm pretty comfortable just about anywhere in Boston, thanks to the anonymity of cab jockeys, but I'd have preferred a route that didn't take in the highlights of Roxbury. Don't get me wrong; I wasn't about to call off the chase. There's nothing like surveillance to make you eager for action. I mean, I didn't want to drive deep into Roxbury, but I had no desire to hang around the Zone looking for Janine forever either. I wanted to track her down now, get this business over with, and start work on finding Valerie, the high-school runaway.

I'm a good driver. I can leave my cab on automatic pilot while I puzzle things out. I wondered about Elsie's "Ask Jerry why she left" remark. Had Jerry driven Valerie away, then hired me to soothe his guilt? Would Valerie run from a rough pass? How shy was she? How grown up? I've seen girls sell their bodies at eleven and brides blush at twenty-eight, so you can't tell. On the dashboard, Valerie's photo, dark and uncommunicative, stood out against the fake grained wood. Between pothole lurches, I grabbed it and tucked it into my purse.

Columbus Avenue doesn't get much in the way of maintenance. Some say that's because Boston is a racist city and nobody cares what happens in the black areas. I suspect it's true. I mean, the Red Sox used to have one black player. They'd get two, they'd trade the old one. Slow white boys were their specialty.

The Sox are getting better, but the Celtics are still one of the palest teams in the NBA.

I composed a blistering mental letter to the Department of Public Works, accusing them of racism in pothole repair. I was glad I wasn't driving a small foreign car. In the dark I couldn't keep an eye on the Chevy and watch for craters at the same time. I hit one the size of a canyon and cracked my skull on the padded roof. I didn't hear any hubcaps fall off, for which I was grateful. Thank God, the guys ahead of me weren't speeding.

If anything, they were driving a little too lawfully for two gents with a hooker between them. No weaving, no sign of the one-handed wheeling required for groping a thigh or hoisting a beer. I wondered if they'd spotted me, but they didn't speed up or turn. I dropped back, took a place in line behind a Pontiac Turbo. But I kept my eyes on that Chevy's tail.

They turned into Franklin Park. I cursed, but followed. Franklin Park was once a well-tended gem in Boston's chain of Emerald Necklace parks. When the whites left the area the money went with them, and the golf course went to hell and so did the zoo. They keep talking about revivals and kite festivals and bringing the park back, but all the cash that goes into the zoo seems to disappear into some construction company's pockets, and the golf course clubhouse has been a burnt-out shell for years.

Courting couples wouldn't dream of nighttime necking in Franklin Park. Franklin Park is where you go to get beaten and raped. Franklin Park is where you go to dump a body out of a car.

Tailing was tougher now because there weren't many cars on the road. I hung way back, just catching the faintest glimpse of the taillights. There was a chance I'd lose him, because the roads in the park twist and turn. But he kept bearing right, and I was pretty sure he'd come out onto the Arborway at Forest Hills.

There was nothing behind me and then there was. The car must have been cruising without lights. It wasn't visible until the driver suddenly switched on his brights. They burned in my rearview mirror, momentarily blinding. I squinted and held up my right hand to shield my eyes from the glare. I shouldn't have taken a hand off the wheel.

It happened fast. I felt the rush of speed as the front bumper hit my rear bumper and carried me forward. I hit the brake, but the cab wasn't in my control anymore. I couldn't look at the rearview mirror and drive and stomp the brake and turn the wheel and yell all at the same time. Reflex took over and then I was off the road weaving through high grass, bumping and thrashing, wrestling the wheel. Abruptly, the extra speed was gone. I braked, but the tree in front was too close. I jerked the wheel as hard as I could, counterclockwise, thinking of Gloria's brand-new cab and Gloria's three huge brothers. Right before impact, I turned the key. The engine died. The tree was too damn close.

I jerked forward but the harness seat belt did its stuff. The noise was immediate and surprisingly soft, a series of slow-motion crunches rather than one tearing crash. The car and the tree shuddered. The tree stayed upright, protruding from the right front fender. The boom box hit the dash, then the floor. It kept on playing. I thought maybe I could send it to some advertising company, like the one that does those wristwatch commercials: Timex keeps on ticking.

I jerked my head to the right. Taillights—not the Chevy's—vanished over a rise, and I hoped they were the lights of the bastard who'd forced me off the road. I fumbled under the seat for the hunk of lead pipe most cab drivers keep as standard equipment. It felt cold and heavy.

I turned off the music, killed the headlights. Showing your emergency flashers in Franklin Park is asking for trouble. I sat and breathed, glad of the air, moved my legs, flexed my arms. My right knee ached. My hands tingled but I thought that was just from squeezing the wheel so hard. I could hear the faint hiss of the radiator, nothing else. I might have been on the moon, not in the middle of a city park. I could see the burnt pillars of the clubhouse.

I groped in my purse, found a ballpoint, and scribbled the license number of the gray Caprice on the back of an envelope. My hand shook, but I got it down. I tested out my voice, then I picked up the speaker and called Gloria.

Eight years ago, a drunk hit my cab, racing a red light at Boylston and Tremont. I broke my nose bouncing off the steering wheel, and I've been a seatbelt fanatic ever since. My nose had already been broken twice before: once when the little boy next door smacked it with a hammer; once when a felon pushed my face into a wall. My friends say my nose has character.

While I waited for Gloria's reassuring voice, I found myself rubbing my nose, running my forefinger down the bridge and over the slight bump. I guess I've gotten fond of its shape.

CHAPTER
11

I missed my Thursday morning volleyball game.

I didn't get home till Thursday morning—half past five to be exact—at which time I passed out kitty-cornered across the bed, fully clothed down to my sneakers. I must have set the alarm from force of habit. When it blared, what seemed like seconds later, I stuck out my right arm to shut down the sucker, regretted the movement instantly, and recalled the accident in full-color, 3-D detail. My left shoulder felt like someone had driven a spike deep into the muscle. My knee throbbed. An angry red welt creased my right forearm where I'd bashed it into the steering wheel. When I shut my eyes I could see flashing yellow lights, hear the cry of piercing sirens.

I slithered across the bed to the phone, dialed Kristy, our captain and best setter, and mumbled my excuses.

I hate to miss volleyball. I don't think I've skipped more than a couple of days in four years. We run a hard, tough game, no beach-blanket bimbo stuff. Major league rules, referee, the whole bit. I love the pace, the speed, the intensity—and I like my teammates. We give it all we've got, and we treat each other well. There's always a slap on the back for a flying leap in a losing cause. It makes the black-and-blue knees and elbows easier to bear.

I curled back into the sheets and slept like the dead.

I forgot to reset the alarm and was almost late for lunch with Preston Haslam. Valerie's dad had left two messages on my answering machine the night before: the first, asking me to get in touch; the second, setting a time and place for a meeting. Compared to his dithery wife, the husband seemed a model of clear thinking.

The only reason I didn't slumber through lunchtime was Twin Brothers Plumbing, who came by bright, early, and noisy. I crept out of bed, gingerly peeled off my dirty clothes, shrugged into a bathrobe that was suddenly getting a good deal of use, and scurried downstairs to the tiny half-bath.

While attempting to take a shower in the sink, I checked out my contusions. In addition to the aching knee and the red welt on my arm, I had a nicely purpling bruise on my left collarbone and a long scratch on my left thigh. I tried to remember when I last had a tetanus shot. I almost dislocated my shoulder trying to inspect it in the five-by-eight-inch mirror over the sink.

Back in my room, I found a roll of Ace bandage in the bottom drawer under a moth-eaten sweater, wrapped it securely around my knee, dressed in a white silk V-neck shirt and jeans tight enough to hold the bandage in place. I didn't have the time or patience to deal with my hair.

When I was two years old, I used to wail whenever my mother approached, comb in hand. My hair was too thick and wild to control without pain. As a teenager, I hated curly hair. I used to roll it wet onto giant orange-juice cans and actually sleep like that till it dried, waking with astounding headaches. I even ironed it a few times. I can still see the look of total disbelief in my mother's eyes as she watched me wielding the iron, my head bent over the ironing board, long red curls splayed out from my nape across its surface, steam rising with the odor of singed hair.

Sleek, straight hair was so damn *vital* then, at what? fourteen? fifteen? Valerie Haslam's age.

Now I find my curly hair a blessing. I wash it and give it a shake or two as it dries. It has a will of its own and it suits me: laziness as a fashion statement.

I surveyed myself in the full-length mirror on the back of my closet door and added Aunt Bea's oval gold locket. I was glad I wasn't meeting Haslam in a posh Back Bay eatery. Chinatown is more my style.

If I hadn't had to park the car, I'd have been early. That's Boston. If you brave the MBTA, you have to allow for the inevitable train breakdown. If you choose your car, you need to search the city for a parking space. It used to be bad, but now, since they've done away with half the legal parking spaces, it's ludicrous. The city's been converting them to pedestrian malls, or—my favorite—Resident Only Parking.

This is how Resident Only Parking operates: There are, say, nine hundred parking spaces in the South End, so the registry issues thirty-six hundred Resident Parking Permits. Works like a charm.

I deserted my Toyota in a loading zone. It was either that or block a fire hydrant.

Chinatown is a scant block from the Combat Zone and a world away. Limping down Kneeland Street, I passed a butcher shop. Duck carcasses hung in the window, meat smoked to a deep maroon, necks elongated, eyes glistening. A jewelry shop featured a carved jade Buddha surrounded by red silk fans. The air smelled of ginger root, scallions, and five-spice powder. The phone booths had curved pagoda roofs.

The Imperial Tea House is big—two floors and a neon sign. Three leather-jacketed Vietnamese teens came out as I entered. They did not hold the door.

I stepped inside, removed my peacoat with a jolt of shoulder pain, hung it on a twisted wire hanger, and jammed it into an already crowded rack. A man approached.

I wouldn't have pulled Haslam out of a file labeled "distraught parents," that's for sure. At first glance, he looked too young to be the father of a teenager. He was maybe an inch taller than me, with medium brown hair, a small patrician nose, full lips. His face was tanned, and his eyes had nice creases in the corners when he greeted me.

I tried to see a resemblance between him and his

daughter. Maybe the eyes. His tortoiseshell glasses made them look smaller than they were.

"Ms. Carlyle?" he said. "Jerry described you. He didn't think I'd have trouble picking you out."

I was glad for the "Ms." I find my prefix situation somewhat ambiguous. I'm not technically Miss Carlyle, having been married. And I'm not Mrs. Anybody, never having taken my ex's last name as my own. And I don't think my marital history should be of any concern to people who don't know me well enough to call me by my first name.

The maître d' asked if we'd like upstairs or downstairs. Haslam said up. The waiter ushered us to a central table. Haslam asked for a booth in the back. He told the waiter he didn't have a lot of time, so I waived the menu and we ordered, agreeing quickly on hot and sour soup, spring rolls, Kung Pao chicken, and spicy green beans with pork.

The waiter left, scrawling characters on a yellow pad, and Haslam did a careful survey of the room. It was two-thirds full, the clientele equally split between Oriental and Occidental. At a table to my right a tight-lipped man and his son argued over car insurance.

"I'm sorry," Haslam said, catching my eye, keeping his voice low. "This seems so—I don't know—crazy. Going to work, going to lunch, with Valerie missing." He shook his head and repeated the word. "'Missing.' It sounds so stupid, so melodramatic." He rubbed his forehead with his hands, circling his temples with his fingertips. "I can't do any good staying home. I know that. This morning I drove around before I went to the office, looking for her. And why would she hang out near my office unless she wants me to find her? And if she wants me to find her, why doesn't she come home?"

He had a faint nervous tic on the left side of his jaw. On closer inspection he fit pretty neatly into the "distraught" category. He just put up a better front than most.

He extended both hands, stared at them like they belonged to somebody else, and folded them on the table. Then he sucked in a couple of deep breaths. "Excuse me," he said, his voice calmer. "I'm Preston Haslam. That's how I meant to start."

His handshake was firm and cool.

He leaned closer to me, spoke softly and quickly. "I'm grateful to Jerry for hiring you. But now that I'm back—I mean, Jerry's a kid. I'd like to join him or replace him or whatever. No conflict of interest. We both want you to find my daughter. I'd just like to, well, take over. His family wouldn't miss the money or anything, but it's not right. They shouldn't be paying for my family. Okay?"

"Did you talk this over with Jerry?"

"Yeah. Sure. Can I write you a check or what? Jerry said five hundred for a retainer." He had his checkbook out on the table. He hunched over it like he was hiding evidence of a drug deal.

"Let's talk first," I said to slow him down. I wondered if he always spoke at top speed or if it was another sign of nervousness. "When did you see Jerry?"

"I see him all the time. He's out in the driveway trying to make his old hulk of a car work. I wave to him in the morning and he's still there at night."

"Do you think he could be feeling, uh, guilty about Valerie?"

His hand hesitated over the checkbook. "Well, if he did, that would make two of us," he said, glancing up abruptly. Beneath the glasses he had soft brown eyes, long-lashed. "Look, you want a drink? I'm going to have a bourbon and water. I don't usually, but—" He waved and the waiter flew over, took my order for a screwdriver—orange juice for breakfast, right?—and Haslam's Jim Beam.

"Why should Jerry feel guilty?" Haslam asked, picking up where he'd left off. "He's a terrific kid, like a brother to Valerie."

I said, "Why do you feel guilty?"

He finished writing, ripped the check out, and replaced the folder in his breast pocket. "Because I didn't know," he said more slowly. "I've been in Chicago the past week, on business."

"Your wife didn't mention it?"

"My wife is not—well, she's not in good health. I try to avoid traveling, but sometimes I have to go."

Our drinks came with the soup. The screwdriver was strong. Haslam drank his bourbon like a thirsty man.

"What is it you do?" I asked. I'm always interested in the occupations of people who can write five-hundred-dollar checks without looking worried, and pay tuition at places like the Emerson.

"Investments," he said. "Stockbroking, analysis. A little work with the commodities market. That's why I had to be in Chicago. It's mostly plodding stuff, but I'm good at it. I can't let this business at home get to me at work," he said as if he was trying to convince himself instead of me. "Oh, hell. I probably should have had you come to the house instead of trying to squeeze this into the workday, but I didn't want to upset my wife. She's feeling very guilty, very depressed. I thought maybe if I handled it here . . . I don't know . . ."

I took another sip of my drink. My interrogation technique can be summed up in three words: Let them talk.

While he talked I watched. He had a trick of fiddling with his glasses, sliding them up and down his nose. His navy suit was expensive, probably custom tailored. He seemed intense, but not worried. I imagine a worried-looking stockbroker would not last long. The glasses gave him a solid, respectable look. Intellectual, but jovial. Good eyes. Long fingers; buffed, manicured nails. Onyx cuff links.

"Do you know why your daughter ran away?" I asked when he seemed to run out of chatter about his job and his wife and how hard this had been on her.

"No idea," he said quickly. Then he hesitated, as if the first had been a knee-jerk response and not what the situation required. He said, "I don't know. Because she wants more attention, I guess. My wife, well, she has health problems. Sometimes, I don't know, I think she's almost jealous of the girls. And she's not strong. She has to rest a lot. I suppose she doesn't really take good care of any of us. Valerie had to take on a lot of responsibility early."

"When did you see her last?"

"What's today? Thursday? A week ago Tuesday. At night. Watching TV in her room. My wife saw her the next morning."

"And hasn't seen her since, Mr. Haslam—"

"Pres, call me Pres, okay?"

"Your daughter's been gone for over a week. Why did it take your wife so long to—"

"Look, she thought Valerie was with her friends, okay? Sherri, that's my little one, said Valerie was staying with a friend at school, and maybe she did for a few days. Maybe she's just with a different friend now."

"Then there wasn't any argument at home, right before she took off?"

"Mathilde says there was no argument. She doesn't argue. And listen, what's important here is finding Valerie, making sure she doesn't get hurt out there. Later, when she's home, we'll deal with whatever upset her so much. You just find her. All this question and answer stuff isn't going to help—"

"Mr. Haslam," I said very quietly, "if you want somebody to find your daughter and not ask questions, you'd better get yourself a bloodhound and give him a shoe to sniff. Investigators ask questions. I've already asked Jerry a few. He doesn't think Valerie ran away. If she didn't, then we have to consider other possibilities. Have you called the police?"

"No," he said. "I, uh, I'd rather not—"

"Your daughter has been gone over a week—"

"I'd rather not," he repeated.

"She's only fourteen years old, Mr. Haslam—"

"Listen," he said flatly. "This isn't the first time." He swallowed hard, avoiding my eyes, slicing his spring roll into tiny bits. "She's run away before."

"But Jerry said—"

"Maybe Jerry doesn't know that much about Valerie," he said. "She presents herself in different lights. She's a good little actress, my Valerie."

"She's run away more than once?"

"Twice before," he said. "The first time she came home on her own. Mathilde thought she might do it again. So she waited. She hoped. You can understand that."

"And the other time—"

He pushed a piece of spring roll around his plate. "The police picked her up."

"In the Combat Zone?"

"How did you—?"

Maybe Jerry knew more than Haslam gave him credit for.

"A lot of kids wind up there," I said.

He rubbed his hand across his forehead like he was trying to ease a headache. The tic in his jaw was more pronounced. "Oh, Christ," he muttered under his breath, "I should have pulled her out of that school."

"The Emerson?"

"Everybody said to get her out of public school. I mean, to listen to people, public schools are hotbeds of drugs and sex and God knows what else. The Emerson is expensive, but they're supposed to take care of the kids. Good care, not expose them to weirdos and perverts."

The waiter brought more food so we were forced into silence. As soon as he left, I prompted Haslam, repeating what he'd said. "Weirdos and perverts?" They weren't words I associated with the Emerson.

He started on the Kung Pao chicken with his knife and fork. I used chopsticks.

"The kids at the Emerson," he said after a swallow, "they look okay. They dress well and they've got good teeth. Money. But they're a fast crowd. And Val tries to keep up. I mean, we're not that rich. We're well off, don't get me wrong. I'm not giving you some wrong-side-of-the-tracks story here. But my dad stocked shelves at a grocery store. I wasn't born to money. I had to work for what I got, and that's not exactly respected at the Emerson. Val always wants to show that she's as good as any of them. And by good, I mean rich.''

"You said 'weirdos and perverts.' You have anybody in mind?''

"I should have yanked her out of there. But her mother likes the place. It's something, to say your kid's at the Emerson. I mean, even at the office—''

"Weirdos and perverts?'' I repeated.

He pushed his plate away. He'd eaten maybe two forkfuls. "Her drama teacher. That's what they call the son of a bitch, a drama teacher.''

"Geoffrey Reardon?''

"You know the name.''

"I went to the school yesterday.''

"I thought the man might be notorious in law and order circles,'' he said.

"Not that I know.''

"She's always staying after school with him.''

"Just the two of them?''

"The drama club. She says.''

"That doesn't seem so bad.''

Haslam glanced at the man discussing auto insurance at the next table as if he might be an undercover FBI agent, and lowered his voice to little more than a whisper. "This may sound dumb—paranoid, even—but that man has got some kind of hold over his students, over my daughter at least. I don't know what he does with them, but it's, well, it's not normal. It's like she was a Hare Krishna or a Moonie or something. She can't come home. She's got rehearsals every day, but there never seems to be a goddamn performance. And she's got extra sessions and mood work and preening in front of mirrors and emoting and sensationalizing every tiny thing in her life."

"Sounds like what a lot of teenagers do anyway," I said.

"He encourages them. The girls. And the pretty boys. He takes photos."

"And you suspect something a little more racy than your old-fashioned drama club?"

"I do."

"But how can you blame Reardon when you say she's run off before?"

"There's always a trigger."

"What was it last time?"

"A fight with a teacher. Valerie likes to be right."

I pursued a slippery green bean around the plate with my chopsticks. "She sounds like a difficult child," I said.

He grimaced. "You have kids?"

I thought of Paolina in Bogota. "No," I said.

"Sometimes Valerie's difficult. Sometimes she's, well, terrific. Perfect. I hate the thought of her out there somewhere, alone. . . ." He lowered his eyes to the tabletop. He wasn't eating, but his hand stayed clenched around his fork.

"I went to see Reardon yesterday," I said.

"What did he say?" Haslam asked sharply.

"He wasn't in."

"The man's nothing but an actor."

"You've met him."

"The Emerson prides itself on close parent-teacher

contact." Haslam didn't try to keep the sarcasm out of his voice. "Whenever I see him he gives me all this soothing bullshit about adolescent rebellion. I think the kids rebel just so he'll approve of them. The man is attractive. The girls chase him. They've all got crushes on him."

"Valerie?"

"I think so. Yes."

"I'll keep that in mind."

"Look, just find my daughter. Whatever you need, I'll cooperate. Mathilde reads the papers, all the sensational stuff about rapes and murders—and, well, she's hysterical. That's not too strong a word for it. She has a vivid imagination, and it's taking over—"

Haslam realized that his voice was getting louder. The insurance advocate was giving him the eye. He took a deep breath and straightened his tie.

"What did Valerie take with her?" I asked.

"I don't know."

"Did you or your wife check her room? Is a suitcase missing?"

"She had her backpack when she left for school. She has so many clothes, I can't tell if anything's gone. I mean, she'd borrow things from other girls at school and lend things. She has an allowance, a generous allowance, so she can choose her own clothes."

"Does she have money other than her allowance?"

"She has a savings account. I don't know if she took her passbook. I'll check on that. I should have done it this morning."

"One more thing," I said. "Your daughter—does she use drugs?"

"No," he said loudly. Then he shook his head.

"Hell," he muttered, "not that I know. I don't know anymore. I don't know. I don't think so."

"And if she ran out of money . . ." I checked my words, continued slowly. It was a hard question to ask a father. "I mean, the police found her in the Zone last time. Was she into prostitution?"

He finished his drink and stared at the empty glass regretfully. "No," he said very softly. "I don't think so. I don't think so." He kept on shaking his head, denying the possibility over and over.

"I'll do my best to find her," I said softly.

"Keep me informed, okay? And let me know if I can do something. Anything. Besides pay you. Is five hundred okay?"

I went through my usual spiel. I charge a daily rate, but missing persons stuff is so dicey that I take something up front, charge expenses, and then it's cash on delivery. A lot.

Haslam passed over the check.

I pulled Valerie's picture out of my wallet. "Is this a good likeness?" I asked.

He looked at it for a long time. "Yes and no," he said. "The last time, when I went to get her, she had gunk all over her face, lipstick, eye stuff." He tapped his finger on the photo's surface. "But most of the time, she looks like this. She was such a beautiful child." He stared hard at the picture, like he might be able to see beneath its surface, read something in his daughter's unresponsive eyes.

He glanced at his watch and hurriedly called for the check. He handed me a business card from a downtown brokerage firm with a familiar name and, apologizing, left before me.

I stayed to drink tea, collect the leftovers in their white goldfish boxes, and investigate the fortune cookies.

One said: "You'll be rich and famous in a far-out profession." The other: "A sense of humor is your greatest asset."

I got to take my choice.

CHAPTER
12

I f you think parking in Chinatown is impossible, try the streets around 40 New Sudbury Street, home of the Area A cops, patrolling Downtown, Chinatown, Charlestown, and East Boston. After cruising a few blocks, competing with the Faneuil Hall tourist brigade, I decided to risk a spot marked POLICE BUSINESS ONLY, FIFTEEN MINUTES MAXIMUM. There is nothing you can get done at the Area A station in less than fifteen minutes.

Up the steps, turn right, turn left. I could have walked the pattern in my sleep, did sleepwalk it often enough during my two-year stint at Area A. The smell—a blend of bad coffee and fear that seems to have soaked into the beige walls and checkered linoleum—brought the memories back, made my shoulders stiffen as though I was wearing the uniform again.

I don't miss it, most of the time.

I didn't recognize the desk sergeant. I almost said "Lieutenant Mooney" when he asked me who I wanted to see. That's how far I'd repressed his suspension. I caught myself and asked for Joanne Triola instead. Joanne came up with me from the Academy. She's better at putting up with guff than I ever was or will be, and as a result she is still a cop, a rising star. The desk sergeant said Detective Bureau, Second Floor.

He gave me a clip-on visitor's pass, and I headed up the stairs. The fifth step was still missing its rubber retread, and the eighth step still creaked if you hit it dead center.

The rookies who'd responded to last night's accident had been strangers from Area D, and matter-of-fact to the point of boredom. The gist of their chat was: What the hell did I expect driving at night in Franklin Park? And couldn't I keep my damn cab on the road?

I don't take kindly to aspersions cast on my driving skills. The three of us did not hit it off.

They'd listened to my forced-off-the-road story with such undisguised skepticism that I'd gone no further. If they didn't believe in the car that shoved me into the tree, how were they going to grasp the news that I'd been tailing yet another car complete with missing witness inside?

I should have told them, I suppose, should have demanded they call in an accident team to check my rear bumper for paint chips, but just as I opened my mouth, the two of them exchanged The Look. You know, the why-do-they-let-these-crazy-broads-out-at-night look. And I'd decided to save my breath.

Joanne, I could talk to.

She was slouched in a chair in the bullpen, a warren of desks that serves as combination typing pool and doughnut dispensary. Every once in a while somebody shrieks about privacy and efficiency and tries to install dividers, but most of the time there aren't that many cops around. They're on the beat, or talking to snitches, or tracking down leads, or growing old in courtrooms waiting to testify about crimes that occurred three and a half years ago.

Today, the bullpen was graced by one old cop named Foley, a desk jockey who'd retired in all but name a couple years back, and a young Hispanic guy who looked eighteen max, but was acting like a cop, pounding away on his typewriter and shooting questions at a young woman in his guest chair. The lady wore black— blouse, skirt, tights, and boots—and handcuffs. I don't know much Spanish but I recognized several words Paolina would not have used in polite conversation.

Joanne was gabbing on the phone, speaking loudly, gesturing freely. She must be almost fifty and she's energetic enough for three normal people. She has a round, gentle face, a puff of graying hair, a ready smile, and one of those laughs that makes people turn around in a restaurant.

She can outscore me on the target range, either hand.

She hung up, glared at the phone, and started dialing again. I cleared my throat and she looked up, a smile breaking across her face.

"Why, it can't be," she said. "Why yes, the height is right. Didn't you used to be a cop?"

"Thanks," I said. "I'd love to sit and chat a while." I slid into her visitor's chair, thankful to get the weight off my knee. It felt stiff and swollen, and I hoped I wasn't going to have to cut off my very best pair of jeans. What I needed was a long soak in a hot tub.

"I'd ask you to join me in a cup of coffee," she said, "but I seem to recall—"

"Still that bad?" I said. The woman in black jumped off her chair and swore in good old Anglo-Saxon. The cop who was booking her chuckled and said her English was getting much better.

"Honest to God, Carlotta," Joanne said, taking no notice of the outburst from across the room, "you stir it with one of those plastic gizmos from McDonald's, and the little spoon dissolves."

"Coke machine work?" I asked.

"What do you think?"

Her phone rang, so I went over to investigate the vending machine, trying not to favor my left leg. The machine blazed with red warning lights that declared it gave no change and was out of every beverage it was supposed to stock. I gave it a gentle kick for the old days. I'd forgotten the crazy rhythm of the bullpen, the counterpoint of bells and questions and typewriters, entrances and exits, long calm afternoons broken by sudden, brutal emergencies.

Joanne was signing off when I came back.

"Jo," I said, "I got run off the road last night."

"Yeah?" she said. "Where?"

"Franklin Park."

Her eyebrows shot up and she grinned. "Way to go," she said. "And lived to tell about it." Then she held up a hand like a traffic cop, requesting silence while she shuffled through a stack of paper.

"Here it is," she said finally. "Area D. You got a big two sentences in the occurrence book."

"The jerks wrote it up," I said. "I'm flattered."

"It's no big deal," she said. "Two sentences."

"Where're they getting the rookies these days?" I asked.

"Well," said Joanne, "with our incredible benefit package and high starting salary we have to fight off those Harvard MBAs."

"Yeah," I said. "I see."

The woman in black rattled her handcuffs and called the Hispanic cop a son of a mangy yellow dog, in both Spanish and English. It was more effective in Spanish.

"You wanna come back?" Joanne asked.

"No, thanks," I said.

She smiled. "So who's after your ass?" she said. "You working a case?"

"Sort of," I said.

"And this is just a social visit, right?" she said.

"I got a license plate," I said. "I was wondering if you could run it." A phone rang somewhere, ten times, twelve times, stopped.

"You give it to the boys last night?" she asked.

"No."

"Carlotta, they may be jerks, but they can run a plate."

"I've got a plate, but it's not the car that rammed me," I said. The phone started up again. Six, eight, ten rings before someone mercifully plucked it off the hook.

She said, "Let me get this straight. You just wrote down a license for the hell of it?"

"Hey, it's connected," I said. The Hispanic cop finished his paperwork and escorted the woman in black to a holding cell. Close up, under her eye makeup, she was a teenager. The right sleeve of her blouse was ripped, and her skinny yellow arm showed needle tracks.

"How?" Joanne asked.

"I'll know once you run it, Jo. Maybe."

"This have to do with Mooney?" she asked, leaning over her desk and getting all quiet and confidential.

God knows what the station house grapevine says about Mooney and me, but I'm sure it's juicier than reality. "Would that make you run the plate any faster?" I asked.

"I'm just curious, you know," she said.

"Seen Mooney?" I asked.

"He's not allowed in. It might be catching."

"I thought he had to come by and testify about something."

"Oh, that," she said, elaborately casual. "That's over at county courthouse."

"What's it about?"

"Confidential?" She shot a careful glance around the bullpen. The old cop, Foley, was learning how to type with two fingers.

"Sure," I said easily.

"Cheating on paid detail," she said.

"Mooney?" I said quietly. The Hispanic cop wandered back to his desk. He propped his feet on his blotter, dialed his phone. Joanne waited until he started talking before she answered, very softly.

"The way I heard it, is somebody offered him five bills to alter records, right after the probe started. It wasn't that obvious. Oblique as hell, really, but Mooney, well, you can imagine."

I felt my stomach muscles unknot. "I knew it," I said. "He frothed at the mouth, right? He's cooperating with Internal Affairs." I smiled and issued a silent apology for my thoughts over the morning *Herald*.

"Keep it down," Joanne said. "He's a perfect witness. These cops are gonna get strung by their thumbs." She walked over to the bullpen's central table, picked up a pink-and-white box, and came back. "Want a doughnut?" she asked.

The box was half-full. Cinnamon and chocolate. I liked glazed and jelly.

"No, thanks," I said. "But there is something else you can do for me, besides running the plate, I mean. I'm looking for a runaway."

"Good luck," she said, her voice back to full volume now.

"A repeater. There ought to be paper," I said. Two cops, one black, one white, came through the swinging doors, supporting a man between them. He could have been drunk or doped or dead. They passed by and the smell made me glad I hadn't taken the doughnut.

"Juvie?" Joanne asked. Nothing seemed to sway her, not the noise, not the smells. I must have been like that once, before I got rid of the badge.

"Yep," I said.

"Probably sealed."

"I don't think it went to court. It's just paper lying around someplace."

"Look, are you helping Mooney?" she asked.

"I'm trying," I said.

She pushed a sheet of paper across the desk. "Write down the plate, and give me the girl's name while you're at it."

"Thanks," I said. "I owe you."

"Say something nice about your local police department," she said with a heartfelt sigh. "We can use it."

CHAPTER
13

My car sported a parking ticket under the windshield wiper. I swear they find me everywhere, those meter maids. I hated the idea of one of them making such an easy score, right in front of the damn station.

A Boston ticket used to be a laugh. You bisected it on the spot, end of crisis. Recently, the traffic cops and the registry have sharpened up their act. You can still rip the tickets, but when you try to renew your driver's license, boy, will you be sorry. Better yet, if you rip five tickets, you can get acquainted with the Denver Boot, a yellow eyesore that instantly converts your car from a means of transportation to a hunk of modern sculpture.

The ticket was a five-buck job. If I'd parked in a lot it would have cost me four easy, so I didn't feel so bad. I'd slip it on Haslam's bill under parking fees.

I checked my watch: 2:05. School in session. Just letting out by the time I motored to Lincoln. Maybe a good time to talk to Mr. Geoffrey Reardon. Not that I put a lot of stock in Haslam's theory. I couldn't see the staid Emerson putting up with a "cult" drama club. On the other hand, there were those photo albums with the girls in leotards.

I tuned the radio to WUMB, 91.9 FM, and came in on Chris Smither singing that the sun was gonna shine in my back door someday.

I patted my knee cautiously and wondered who I could call who owned a functional bathtub and wouldn't misunderstand a request to use it. God, I ought to belong to some whoop-de-do health spa instead of the Y. I could waltz into, say, La Pli in Harvard Square, and get my aches pampered and petted and Jacuzzied. Sure thing, girl, I told myself. Membership at La Pli probably cost more than my rent. And in my jeans, with my hair wild, I looked more like a candidate for Madame Floozey's massage parlor.

Used to be I could call Mooney. Back when we worked together, he'd have loaned me his key, no questions. But now there's his mom who probably wouldn't understand, but would think she did.

I let my mind wander to Sam Gianelli. His place at Charles River Park has a great bathtub, a giant bathtub, a queen of bathtubs, a five-by-five blue-tiled sunken square. I tried to imagine my approach: "Sam, it's me, Carlotta. Yeah. I know I screwed up your life and you never want to see me again—but could I use your tub?''

Maybe I could rent one of those hooker hotel rooms for an hour. "Just yourself, lady?" the sleazebag on the desk would inquire. The thought of the bathtub in a place like that made me itch. Oh, God, let the Twin Brothers put my tub back in.

There was always Gloria's room at the back of the garage, but, shit, all those pulleys and bars and stuff. I've heard about these places where you can rent a hot tub for an hour, but it seems like something you ought to do with somebody else, a social occasion calling for a date and a bottle of wine. It also seems much too "California" for a Bostonian. Bostonians are more aware of social diseases than social occasions.

I parked the Toyota under a cherry tree just beginning to bud. It wasn't green yet, but it had turned that fuzzy kind of gray that promises green. The wind was bitter, but the Emerson's campus was calm, sheltered by pines. Kids chattered as they walked to class, yanking on mittens, tightening scarves.

I stuck my hands in the pockets of my coat and started off toward Reardon's office.

I saw Elsie McLintock first, then Jerry Toland, both standing in the middle of the soccer field, waving their arms at each other. I couldn't hear them clearly, but Jerry's voice was raised and angry. I detoured.

The minute Elsie saw me, she practically ran. Jerry flicked a glance over his shoulder, called out to Elsie, then turned back to me. He strolled over, unhurried, feet shuffling through the damp grass, hands in his pockets. His mouth was slightly puffy, healing nicely. He wore khaki slacks and a white knit shirt with yellow stripes that looked expensive and warm. A yellow windbreaker was tied across his shoulders by the sleeves.

"Hi," he said, leaning down to pick up a soccer ball someone had abandoned in the grass. "That is you, isn't it?"

This from a kid who'd seen me in my cab driver outfit and my bathrobe. "It's me," I reassured him. "What's with Elsie?"

He shrugged, dismissing her. "Oh, you know. She doesn't think I should have hired you, and everything." He started kicking the ball around, standing in place, bouncing it off one knee then the other.

"Me in particular?" I said.

"Anybody."

"Why?" I asked.

The ball got away. He retrieved it, started the game over. "She's a pain in the ass, you know. That's why. Hell, I don't know."

"You think she knows where Valerie is?"

"Elsie?" He flashed me a grin. He'd kneed the ball five times in a row. He had good balance. "No way."

"Why? Elsie's her best friend, right?"

"Right," he said.

"Could you just hold on to the ball for awhile?" I said.

He took a step toward me. "Elsie blabs, you know. If she had a line on anything, half her friends would know, and everybody'd be yapping about it. Valerie's not dumb enough to tell Elsie."

This kid on the soccer field had a lot more confidence than the one who'd hid in my cab and bled in my kitchen. From the way he talked about her, Elsie was not Jerry's favorite person.

He said, "Elsie says I just hired you because you're, uh, you're a woman," he said. It took me a minute but I finally caught on. This *kid* on the soccer field was flirting with me.

"You know," Jerry said, looking me over from top to tail, "they don't allow blue jeans."

"Huh? Who? The Kremlin?"

"On campus. The Emerson doesn't allow blue jeans."

"Yeah," I said, "but I don't work for them."

"You look great," he said. He fired the soccer ball at me, hard. I caught it and fired it back. Reflex. I should have held it. The puppy wanted to play.

"Good toss," he said. "How old are you, anyway?" He took another step forward. He was my height. I should have worn heels. My hair in a bun. A raging-hormone repellent spray.

"I could be your mom," I said sternly, biting the inside of my cheek to keep from laughing, "if I'd started early."

"Oedipus, right?" he said.

Ah, the benefits of a classical education, I thought.

"Can it," I said elegantly. "Look, I work for you. Or I did. Now I work for Preston Haslam."

"Mr. Haslam?" That took him back a step.

"We met for lunch. He's my client now."

"I thought I was your client. I thought you said—"

I said, "He didn't talk to you about it?"

"He asked me about you, but geez—" The little kid was back. Even his posture was different. He was the younger brother of the guy who'd been coming on to me a minute ago. "I mean, I suppose it would be okay. My folks are giving me kind of a hard time, you know. They say save my bucks for college. I'm not sure I want to go to college in the first place, you know. It seems kind of dumb. But I've got plenty of money if I want to go. I don't see what their problem is."

"I thought you and Haslam had settled it," I said. "I took his check, but I can rip it up."

"Hey," Jerry said, "that reminds me. I owe you some bucks. Cab fare, right, and the five for the sandwich. Man, that saved my life." He was digging in his pockets while he spoke. He pulled out a gold money clip in the shape of a dollar sign, peeled off one of a wad of twenties. "Keep the change," he said. "For the iodine and stuff."

I didn't raise a hand to take it. "If you're my client, it'll be on your bill," I said. "Are you my client?"

He crumpled the twenty in his hand. "Let me get it straight, okay? Either way, whoever pays, you're gonna find her, right?"

"I'm going to try."

"Can I think about it? Like, don't rip up Haslam's check, but don't rip up that contract I signed either."

"I can leave it like that for a day or two."

"Good," he said. "I need a little time."

"I need a few answers."

"That's all you've been doing, asking questions. I'm gonna be late for math."

"That's what you hired me for, to ask questions."

"Right." He didn't know what to do with his hands, so he started bouncing the soccer ball again.

"Stop it," I said. He tossed me the ball and I held it.

"Want to play tackle?" he said.

"Want to grow up?" I snapped. He fiddled with the sleeves of his windbreaker, and I was sorry I'd raised my voice. God, I don't know what people expect from teenagers. One day sex is secret, the next day it's dirty, the next it's forbidden, and then you get a marriage license and it's a joyful, meaningful experience. Right.

"What can you tell me about the drama coach?" I said.

"Reardon? He's a slug."

"Really?"

"I mean, I don't know. I don't take his class."

"Valerie does."

"Oh, yeah, she thinks he's great, you know. She's always over there with him."

I thought I heard jealousy in the last remark.

"You think she's interested in him as more than a teacher?" I said.

"No way. The guy must be thirty." He said "thirty" like you'd say "embalmed."

"Was she interested in anybody?" I asked.

"Nah."

"In you?"

"Nah." He scuffed the grass with his right sneaker.

"I heard you liked her, as more than a friend."

"Elsie, right? The stupid bitch." He mumbled the last part under his breath.

"You saying Elsie made it up?" I said.

He sat abruptly on the grass, collapsing like somebody had opened a valve and let the air out. He was the kid in the back of the cab again, scared and lonely. He bit his lower lip, winced at the pain.

I glanced around. Two girls in identical red sweaters stood near the flagpole, out of earshot. The wind whipped their skirts and their hair, but they didn't seem to feel it, deep in the exchange of confidences. I felt it. My knee throbbed. I lowered myself onto the thick, damp grass that smelled of pine needles.

"I shoulda told you before," Jerry said. "Oh shit. I was—I am—so goddamned stupid. I'm sorry. Valerie and me, we were, you know, just fooling around last week, back behind the math building, telling jokes and stuff, and then we were, well, fooling around, you know, and we started hugging and then I kinda kissed her and it was fine, and then we went a little further and she just totally freaked."

"That's the last time you saw her?"

"That's the last time I saw her," he repeated, hanging his head. He looked like he'd confessed to a capital crime.

"What do you mean by a little further?" I asked.

"You know," he said, looking at anything but me.

"Intercourse?"

"Shit. Behind the math building? No way. I just unbuttoned her blouse and stuff. That's all. I mean, she freaked. I didn't even see anything."

I sighed. "That's it?"

"That's it."

"No more true confessions?"

"Honestly, that's it."

"Okay."

"Ms. Carlyle?"

"Yeah."

He pulled a clump of grass out by the roots. "When you find her, tell her I'm sorry. Tell her I'm just goddamned sorry."

I left him sitting cross-legged in the middle of the soccer field, getting grass stains on his nice khaki pants.

CHAPTER
14

Reardon's office stood open and empty, so I asked a passing student to point out the little theater. She clutched her books and gave hesitant directions studded with "ers," "ums," "I guesses," and "you knows," finally mentioning a set of stained-glass windows, round like portholes, and patterned in blue doves with scarlet eyes. I saw those and made for them.

It was pitch dark inside double doors that closed behind me with a whoosh. A class was on stage—small, maybe fifteen students. The stage lights blazed, but the auditorium was black, so I crept forward and grabbed a seat, a secret audience.

Once my eyes adjusted, I had no trouble understanding Jerry's jealousy or getting a fix on Haslam's rumors. Geoffrey Reardon was, to put it simply, gorgeous. Sprawled on the stage floor with one knee bent, one leg extended, leaning back on his palms, he'd stationed himself under a baby spot that haloed his hair. Outside fairy tales, not many people have golden hair. It's straw or yellow, sandy or badly bleached. Reardon's hair belonged in an art museum; it was Rembrandt-burnished gold.

He had a sharp profile, a chiseled nose—and believe me, I'm rarely tempted to use the word "chiseled" in that context—a mustache a shade darker than his hair, great teeth. Full front, his face was broad, with high cheekbones, and a genuine Kirk Douglas chin cleft. His circle of surrounding students was mainly female—surprise, surprise—and they stared at him with spaniel eyes.

Much like my own, I thought ruefully, glad of the protective dark.

Why, I wondered, was this breathtaking specimen not on some larger stage? In front of cameras? Earning a fortune churning out TV commercials, modeling Jockey shorts if he couldn't act at all?

I took time out to regulate my breathing and to scold myself for assuming that Reardon's looks, surely not his fault, were his stock in trade. I was not going to cast him as a bimbo. Not before I spoke to him.

He rose in one smooth motion and the kids, in feeble imitation, stood too. They did stretching exercises in a set pattern everyone seemed to know. I felt like joining in—that is, all of me except my aching knee felt like joining in. At a signal, the kids broke rank and started moving on their own. Some did jerky rap-dance steps, some balletic leaps and whirls. A dark-haired boy vaulted an imaginary horse. A girl with long, dark hair tried a cartwheel. She wore tights and a big shirt that threatened to slide up over her bra.

Occasionally, Reardon, prowling the stage restlessly, would yell, and all movement would cease. Then he'd say something, and they'd start again, dancing and spinning and jumping.

It was fun to watch, this game of frozen tag, but it could have used music. To tell the truth, I couldn't figure the exercise out. The kids seemed to enjoy it. It was a far cry from my high-school memories of rigid desks, forced motionlessness, and silence.

Sometimes Reardon joined the dance, as if he had too much energy to stop himself. His movements were stunning, exciting, abrupt. One moment he was still, then he'd erupt, then the stillness again, making me doubt he'd moved at all. He wore a turquoise cotton knit sweater, khaki pants, and white running shoes. His body was slight, but hard. His hair gleamed.

Had Valerie been part of this class? Had she moved in circles, leaps, or stutters?

He motioned and they circled, touching hands, murmuring, the first and only hint of "cult." Then the kids turned and vanished into the bordering black curtains. Alone on stage, Reardon executed a lazy dance step to unheard music.

I could have watched him for hours. I licked my lips and cleared my throat.

He turned like a cat. "Somebody out there?"

I made my way past rows of quiet blue velvet chairs. "Hi," I said.

"Hello." He looked relieved, glad I wasn't somebody else. His brow furrowed attractively. I wasn't a teacher he knew. Too old for a student. He smiled. It seemed flirtatious, but that could have been me.

If I'd been fifteen, I'd have rolled over and died.

"Uh, can I help you?" he said.

"I left you my card," I said firmly, thankful I was not fifteen.

He was beautiful. It wasn't the lights or anything. He glowed. He probably caused traffic accidents when he went out to get the mail.

I said, "I left my card on your desk. Carlotta Carlyle. The private investigator."

He jammed his hands into his pockets and smiled less comfortably. "Oh, yeah. I remember now. I don't see many cards like that. So it's not a joke, huh?"

His voice told me why he hadn't advanced professionally. Speech teachers might have tried, but nobody'd pried all of New Jersey out of that voice. Worse, it was high and reedy. In the days of silent film, he might have rivaled Valentino. Today, he'd have to do spaghetti westerns and get them dubbed.

In some ways his voice was a relief. He didn't distract me as much. I find ugly men with great voices more attractive than great-looking men with icky voices.

"You don't fit my image," he said.

"You don't fit mine," I said.

We looked at each other. He was at stage level and I was two and a half feet below.

"Stairs?" I asked.

He leaned down. "I'll give you a hand up," he said.

I didn't have a chance to say no. When somebody extends his hand like that you think he's going to shake. It's practically reflex, you stick your own out. Next thing I knew I was on stage next to the man and he was grinning. I wondered if he practiced that move on his girl students.

He was maybe two inches shorter than me. He had muscles.

"So what can I do for you?" he said. I got the feeling he'd preferred me on lower ground.

"Is there someplace we can talk?" I said. The view from the stage was weird. I couldn't even see the seat I'd occupied so recently. Other eyes could be out there in the dark.

He checked his watch. "Here or my office?"

"Your office," I said.

"I don't have a lot of time."

"Me either," I said, which was a lie.

He led the way behind black curtains to a metal door and shoved it open with one shoulder, ushering me through. The noise of laughing, chattering kids was deafening. The theater must have been soundproofed. I recognized the hallway outside Reardon's office.

He closed the door behind me, indicated the chair in front of his desk, and sat in the one behind it. The manuscript on his blotter was gone. The split-leaf philodendron had gotten a much-needed drink.

"I can give you fifteen minutes," he said.

I remembered the stash of Wild Turkey in his bottom drawer.

He spread his elbows on the desk and formed his

joined fingers into a pyramid. "I don't mean to be rude," he said looking me straight in the eye. "I have another class. And then rehearsal."

His eyes were Paul Newman blue. "They keep you busy," I said.

"Incredibly. They seem to think I need no preparation time, that I just crank the stuff out. It's exhausting."

Playing frozen tag with fifteen-year-olds didn't look like ditch-digging to me. "I saw part of your class," I said.

"That's a good group. Very fluid. Open."

Fluid? Open?

"Is Valerie in that class?" I asked.

"Valerie?" he said.

"Valerie Haslam."

"Is that what this is about?" he asked. "This investigator stuff? Valerie? I heard she'd run off."

"Who from?"

"Gossip and rumor. It's how I get most of my news."

I nodded, and he gave me a smile that generated heat. He sat up straighter, and his whole manner seemed to change. He started talking eagerly, as if he were glad to see me.

"Valerie's not in the advanced group," he said. "No way. She's part of my nightmare class." He had a trick of speaking very softly, confidingly, drawing the listener nearer. This listener didn't mind. His voice sounded better soft.

He probably knew that.

"The counseling department," he said, "such as it is, has decided that kids needing a few easy credits, especially kids who act out in other classes, need drama in their lives. They ought to send them to woodworking, math, science, teach them a little discipline. I don't want them."

I had the feeling I was not the first to hear this little outburst. "Troublemakers?" I inquired sympathetically, while thinking to myself that this man wouldn't know a troublemaker if he tripped over one. Let him go to Paolina's school for a few days. Let him meet nine-year-olds with knives.

He sighed. His mustache had not a waxed hair out of place. "I was going to put a picture of the Statue of Liberty on my office door with the caption: 'Send me your drugged, your weird, your outcasts, yearning to leave school.'"

He waited for me to smile my appreciation of his cleverness, then went on: "Oh, they're not all bad. They're harmless kids, really, most of them. Valerie's very sweet. Open, no. Getting her to move was like pulling teeth at first. They're so self-conscious, these kids. I used to see her in the hallways, walking next to the lockers, maybe an inch away from them, staring straight ahead. Scary. She was very closed when the class started, but there was something there, something strange, even wild, secretive. I thought she had depth—and now . . ."

"Now?" I prompted.

"Well, I guess her running away proves it."

"Proves what?"

"That she's not as ordinary as she seems, not like every-humdrum-body-else. Maybe that she's synthesizing her experience, creating her own art—"

"By running away?"

"Look," he said, "I've been here four years. We've had two suicides, God knows how many pregnancies, more runaways than I can count. This place may look like heaven, but it's not."

The way he said it, it seemed like a direct warning: Things are not as they seem. I couldn't get a fix on him. His self-conscious artiness, his set phrases and catch-words were like a foreign language. And he was such a performer, using his entire body for the emphasis his voice couldn't quite provide.

"Do you have any idea where Valerie might be?" I asked.

"No."

"Why she went?"

"No."

There was a faint hesitation this time. He smiled at me, as if we were playing a game and he knew the rules and I didn't.

"I heard you were her favorite teacher," I said.

"Really?" He pushed his hair back off his forehead. "I'm flattered. I thought she was starting to get into the movement games, the exercises. She has a very soft voice, not a good stage voice, but she has a presence. Her mime is exciting, even when it's technically flawed."

"Was she in any of your after-school productions?"

"Nothing with a speaking role. But we did some improvisational pieces in the fall, experimental stuff, and, yes, I think she was involved in one or two of those. She moves well. But I didn't know I was her favorite teacher. She doesn't even hand her work in on time."

"So if she told her family that she was staying after school for drama club—"

"Recently? Then she would have been lying." He smiled, a wonderfully warm, flirtatious smile that looked as if it had been practiced in a dozen mirrors. "Acting, maybe."

"I imagine a lot of the girls have crushes," I said.

"What can you do?" he said smugly.

I thought of a few things—like not batting your eyelashes so shamelessly, wearing your clothes a little looser, not posing in the sunlight . . .

"They express their admiration in giggles," he continued. "I have taught enough giggling teenagers to last me a lifetime. I won't miss it."

"You're leaving." I said. Not a question, but a statement.

"I hope and pray this will be my last year."

"Another teaching job?" I asked.

"God forbid. I have had teaching up to here and then some." He smiled again. This one was a variation on the friendly flirtatious one. More sidelong. Smile number two.

"I may take some time off," he continued. "Maybe dance instead of act. I need to get back to performing. Make the New York scene before I get hopelessly old and stale. I hope this will be my last year of giggling misfits."

Given his voice, dance would be a good field. God, he could just stand still. Movement would be extra.

"Then I have this play," he said eagerly. "This thing I wrote. It's been going no place forever, but I'm going to open it up, turn it into a screenplay. I may have some financial backing. I'm a good director. I'd like to do my own script, but you need clout for that. Hollywood is so uncertain." He nodded a few times, staring at the ceiling, seeing something up there that I couldn't.

Hooray for Hollywood, I thought. Why should it be different?

"You said Valerie handed in her assignments late," I said.

"Oh, sorry. Yeah. Yes, she did."

"All of them?"

"I don't give much written work. That's why the counselors sic the losers on me. But they all have to keep a diary, a kind of interior monologue, throughout the class, and I give specific assignments from time to time. The kids never know when the diary's going to be collected. Otherwise, they'd wait until the day before it's due and write a whole semester's worth of bilge in one night. I hate it when it takes longer for me to read the tripe than it took them to write it." Charming smile number three.

"An interior monologue?" I said.

"Their thoughts about the school experience, about themselves, about each other, about me. I try to make them bring their own experiences to acting, so they have to be aware of their emotions. And by the time I get them, by the time they're teenagers, they're already so caught up in *not* showing their feelings. For the boys in particular, even acknowledging emotion is hard."

His hands flew as he spoke, very expressive hands, fingers fully extended. His eyes, open very wide, never left my own. I felt like I was watching a performance given especially for me.

"Do you have the diaries for Valerie's class?" I asked.

He thought it over. "I collected them a few weeks ago."

"Valerie's?"

"Hers was late."

"Could I have a look at it?"

Smile number four, apologetic, but sincere. "I'm sorry, but one of the few things I make a point of is absolute privacy. Otherwise I'd never get them to explore their minds, would I? They know the diary's a safe place to bring their thoughts."

"It might give me an idea of where she's gone."

"Sorry. I just can't do it." His eyes went to a drawer in his desk. I remembered the notebook with the rotten handwriting. Dammit, Valerie's might have been the next one in the pile. "Look," he said, "If there's anything in Valerie's diary about running away, about a special place, anything like that, I'll call you. I have your number."

"When?" I asked.

"You really think this might help?"

"Yes," I said.

"As soon as I can. I've got a lot of stuff on right now, but maybe I can find time tonight. No guarantee."

"The girl's been missing a week," I said.

"And you're looking for her," he said. "How on earth did you get to be a private investigator?"

"I was a cop," I said in a tone that usually kills conversation about what I want to be when I grow up.

"Oh."

"You mentioned the guidance department. Who was Valerie's guidance counselor?"

"She didn't have one." Reardon leaned back complacently. "She never went. Very intelligent decision on her part."

"You don't think she needed guidance?"

"Not the kind they give. They're not therapists, they're high school guidance counselors. They've got slots and they stick kids in them. All they care about is where you go to college. They guide you to a college, period. They don't want to talk. They don't listen."

"But you do."

"Valerie never confided in me, not in words."

"Without words, then," I said. "What did you see in Valerie?"

He paused, seemed to give the qustion some thought. "I don't know. A kind of desperation, maybe. Who knows if I saw what was there? Or what she meant me to see."

I wondered if this guy ever saw anything beyond himself reflected in other people's eyes.

"About tonight," he said, smiling, flirting. "Those diaries. I'll really try to get back to you. Is the number on your card home or office?"

"Both," I said.

There was a knock on the door and a soft voice said, "Geoff, you in there?"

Reardon checked his wristwatch. "I'm late," he said, standing and waiting for me to precede him out of the office. He made quite a production out of locking his door, patting the key in his pants pocket.

The girl in the hallway was more than pretty, with silky blonde hair and a glossy pink leotard. She took his arm to lead him to the stage. Very touchy-feely, this drama coach. Damn friendly, these kids and their teachers.

I watched them disappear down the hall and wondered if the initials "GR" on the back of Valerie's photo stood for Geoffrey Reardon.

I took a few steps and my knee almost buckled. I wondered if the extravagance of the Emerson ran to hot tubs for the gym.

CHAPTER
15

I made it home by four-thirty. The plumbers had not installed a tub. Undeterred by the gaping hole that yawned in its place, they had already knocked off for the day—and Roz was nowhere to be found. The red light on my answering machine flashed, so I sank into a chair, pressed the button, and listened to Mooney's deep voice rattle off a phone number and ask me to return his call. The number wasn't his home phone.

I got a can of Pepsi out of the refrigerator, gulped enough to make my nose tickle, and dialed.

"Mooney? Yeah, hang on a minute," the male voice said. There had been background noises on the tape;

these were more distinct: the clink of glasses, the enthusiastic patter of a TV sports commentator.

"Carlotta?" Mooney said after a long wait.

"Yeah. What's up?"

"Meet me for a drink," he said. "Come on."

A bar. Of course. The guy answering the phone hadn't given the joint's name but a lot of bars didn't. That way customers could give out the phone number to suspicious wives and business partners.

"Come on," Mooney insisted, and I agreed. I thought if he'd taken to spending his afternoons in bars, I ought to see how he was doing.

Al's, an Irish pub in Brighton, wasn't far away. I gave my hair a quick brush, rubbed my aching knee, and left.

Inside, Al's was dark wood and cool, but that was about all you could say on the positive side. The red leather bar stools were cracked, the long wooden bar warped, the linoleum patchy and yellowed with age. Al's solution to his wear-and-tear problems seemed to begin and end with dimming the lights. You could barely see, what with the haze of cigarette smoke.

Mooney was on the far left of the bar with three empty seats between himself and the next customer. The place wasn't crowded. The few patrons stared up at the big-screen TV, mesmerized by college basketball. Mooney's shoulders were hunched. He wore jeans and a navy sweater.

I didn't think there was another woman in the place. It was so dark I couldn't really tell.

I tapped Mooney on the shoulder and we adjourned to a table. He already had a Molson's, and I ordered one of the same.

"You getting anywhere? You find the broad?" He asked as soon as the bartender was out of earshot.

"I'm not sure," I said.

"Sorry," he said. "Broad. I'm not supposed to say that, right?"

I gave him an update on my progress, bare bones, definitely not the way he'd taught me to report. I'm not sure why I didn't fill him in on all details, but maybe it was that I didn't want him out chasing Janine. He'd missed a patch shaving, and I wasn't sure how many beers he'd downed. So I gave him the short form.

If he hadn't been drinking he'd probably have noticed its sketchiness.

"Carlotta," he said, tracing a wet circle on the wooden table. "Look, maybe you should just forget about it."

"If it's the money—" I began.

"It's the damn review board. Who says they'll take her word? A hooker's testimony isn't worth shit. Maybe they'll think I threatened her, bribed her? I mean, even with a witness, unless the damn knife turns up—"

"We'll take it one step at a time, Mooney, right?"

"Sure," he said after a long pull at his beer bottle. He had a glass, but he seemed to have forgotten about it.

"I mean, maybe the woman knows where the knife is," I said.

"Maybe you ought to forget about it."

"Nah," I said. "I'm feeling lucky."

He said, "I'm thinking of resigning."

I'm thinking of swimming the English Channel. I'm thinking of entering a Tibetan monastery. I'm thinking of running for President. Any of them seemed more likely statements than the first. Maybe I hadn't heard him right.

"Mooney," I said. "For Christ's sake—"

"No," he said. "Listen to me. I've been doing a hell of a lot of thinking, and I keep seeing that guy, that Vietnamese guy. He's still in intensive care. I mean, why the hell did I hit him so damn hard, you know?"

"He could have killed you, Mooney."

"There was a time I'd have talked to the guy. I'd have found a way to stop him without sending him to the hospital. I'd have—Hell, maybe I've been a cop too long, you know. You get—different. You start thinking differently. About people."

I'd spent six years teasing Mooney about leaving the force, egging him on even, because it seemed so impossible. Now—

"Mooney," I said quickly, "you used to tell me if all the good cops left—"

"Shit, Carlotta, somebody'll do the job. Maybe it shouldn't be me anymore. Maybe I'm not one of the good guys anymore. Maybe I'm what the papers say, a racist, a Southie Irish bigot. Maybe it's part of me, the way I grew up. I remember there wasn't a kid different from me in my whole school. All Irish Catholic. And I keep thinking about that guy—I mean, I don't have a whole helluva lotta pleasant memories of Vietnam. And I can't remember what I was thinking about when he came at me. I mean, maybe I had some kind of flashback. Maybe I thought, you know, he was the goddamn enemy or something. I don't know."

The bartender came within hailing range and Mooney waved a finger.

"Want another?" Mooney asked.

"No."

"I hate to drink alone," he said. "But I manage."

I didn't respond and he ordered two beers. Maybe he intended to drink them both.

"I mean," Mooney said. "I keep thinking if the guy hadn't been Vietnamese—"

"You said you forgot the language."

"That's what I said."

"Not true?" I asked.

"I don't know. I saw him coming at me and—I don't think about the time I was over there much, Carlotta, but sometimes I wake up sweating and I—"

"What?"

"Shit, I can't talk about this," he said. "I'm sorry. How's Paolina doing? How's—"

"Mooney," I said slowly, "you remember when I shot that guy in the Zone, before I left the force?"

"Yeah," he said. "I remember."

"And you sent me to Dr. Warner?"

"Yeah," he repeated.

"That was a good thing to do. I don't think I ever thanked you for it."

He set his half-empty beer down with a heavy thud. "You think I need a shrink," he said.

"I think you need to talk to somebody who knows how to help. The department's got people like that. I'd like to help you, Mooney, but all I can say is I don't want you to stop being a cop, and even if you fire me I'm going to keep on looking for this hooker because I've known you a long time, Mooney, and—shit . . ." I took a gulp of the second beer, the one I hadn't intended to drink.

Neither of us said anything for a while. The drone of

the sports commentator got louder. The score was tied and the jerk was going into raptures at the thought of a second overtime.

"I'm sorry about my mother," Mooney said.

I took in a deep breath. "Forget it," I said.

"She just doesn't understand—" he began. "Hell," he said under his breath, "I don't understand either."

CHAPTER
16

So how the hell's your knee?"

Those were the first words out of Gloria's mouth when I limped into G&W's late that night, which is why I adore that woman. None of this "What did you do to my cab?" business. No bemoaning what can't be changed.

She had the phone tucked between her shoulder and one of her chins and was busily scribbling an address down with one hand and hanging onto the microphone with the other.

"Get me a cab at 124 Emory," she crooned into the mike. "Come on, boys, pick it up now, pick it up. And be careful. I understand it's slippery at the corner of Comm. Ave. and Allston."

I grinned. In cab talk, "slippery" means the cops have set up a speed trap.

A metallic voice responded: "335, Gloria, I've got it. Five minutes."

"Sit down," she said, replacing the receiver. "Take the weight off."

I sank into the guest chair, forgetting for once to check for cockroaches. I hate the idea of sitting on a cockroach. Nothing squished beneath me.

"Knee's not bad," I said. "But I wish I'd been driving my own car."

"Wishes don't get you shit, you know," Gloria said, punching buttons on her console and biting into a Hostess cupcake. "It happened. It's over. You're sitting here, not lying in some hospital, so you be grateful."

Gloria has a certain authority when she talks like that. I've never heard her version of the car crash that put her in the wheelchair, but she and hospitals are no strangers.

"You want a cupcake?" she asked. She had a whole carton of them, twelve packages, two to a package, squatting on one corner of her desk. "They got cream in the middle," she said.

"No, thanks." Normally I love junk food, but I can't eat with Gloria. I just sit back and marvel.

"The insurance is paid up," she said, separating cellophane from the chocolate frosting with the squiggle on top. "You're bonded. I hate having a cab off the road, but Sam said to go ahead and lease one. Hackney Bureau'll transfer the medallion."

"You told Sam," I said.

"She had to, didn't she?" The voice came from the

doorway leading to the garage, but I didn't have to turn around to see who it was.

Not only hadn't I looked for cockroaches, I hadn't checked for fancy cars outside. He couldn't have been standing there long. I'd have felt his eyes.

"Hi, Sam," I said.

He looked like he'd stopped by on his way to someplace else, wearing an expensive gray suit, a white shirt, and a patterned tie with glints of blue and green. I didn't notice the clothes right away. When I did, I wondered if there was some woman waiting for him out in that Mercedes or BMW, and I swallowed hard.

Sam's not stop-your-heart gorgeous, not like Geoffrey Reardon, but he's the right height and the right build. He's got a strong, bony face, dark eyes and hair, a stubborn chin, and he does something to me, just standing across a room, that most men can't do no matter how close they come.

"Carlotta," he said. It came out flat, an acknowledgment of my presence, nothing more.

"Sorry about the cab," I said.

He had Gloria's big ledger under his arm. He's the partner who keeps the books, and he stops in from time to time to pick up the records. I shot a reproachful glance at Gloria, who could have warned me. She was communing with Hostess.

"Nice blouse," he said. I couldn't remember what I was wearing. I knew I'd changed at home after substituting hot compresses for the longed-for bath. I remembered feeding the cat, the bird, admiring one of Roz's incomprehensible paintings. My turquoise shirt, that's what I'd chosen. Tucked into black jeans.

"Nice suit," I said.

His face had that clean, just-shaven glow, and I thought I could catch a hint of his after-shave, but it was probably just my nose playing tricks—and my memory.

To tell the truth, standing in the doorway under the light from the bare hanging bulb, he looked like a goddamn knight in shining armor. But did I feel like a damsel in distress? Nope. We six-foot-one-inch women rarely do. Glass slippers don't come in size eleven.

There was one of those silences. I could hear Gloria demolishing cupcakes. Sam and I have too much to say to each other, and not enough. I left a message on his answering machine six months ago. A very inadequate message.

"Maybe you're getting to be bad luck," he said.

"I hope not," I said. "I don't mean to be."

More silence.

"Your cop buddies gonna get the guy who hit you?" he asked.

"Maybe," I said. "You know how it is."

"If you got a license plate, I know somebody who can run it down," he said.

Sam Gianelli is the son of a Boston Mob boss. He has ways of getting information that I don't even want to think about. If your name is Gianelli in this town, people tell you things. Strangers fall on their faces doing you favors.

"I'd like to do it," he said.

Maybe he had a couple more lines at the corners of his eyes. Maybe I was just searching for flaws.

Gloria stopped chewing long enough to say, "Of course she got a plate. She's got good eyes and she uses them. Here, write it down on this." She stuck a stub of pencil in my hand and slid a card across her desk. I wrote down the number of the gray Caprice, feeling like I ought to explain that it wasn't really the car that had run me off the road, knowing that I didn't want to start a discussion. Not about Mooney's problems. Not with Sam.

Gloria clicked her tongue impatiently, waiting for me to hand the card to Sam, or for him to cross the room and take it. We must have been eight, ten feet apart.

"Well, shit," she said finally, reaching for the card and reading it aloud. "It's 486-ITO. Got that? Mass. plate, right?"

"Right," I said.

"I'll see what I can do," Sam said.

"Thanks," I said.

He turned and went out the door, and I started breathing again.

The phone rang. Gloria scribbled, sang an order over the mike to pick up a Dr. Bennett on Peterborough Street. She blew cupcake crumbs off her desk. Then she motored her chair halfway around the desk, leaned forward, and tapped me on the shoulder. "Wake up," she said sharply. "That wasn't so damn bad, was it? You could have moved your ass and given him the damn card, you know?"

"You could have told me he was here, Glory."

"Yeah, but then you'd have walked out, right?"

"Maybe."

"Can't hide from him all your life, babe."

"Who's hiding?" I said.

Gloria shot me a cream-filled smile. She has this incurable, romantic, happily-ever-after streak that fascinates me. I mean, if working at Green & White Cab in a wheelchair doesn't knock that kind of crap out of you, what will?

"Look," I said, "I want a cab."

"Shit," she said. "One thing about you, Carlotta, you never quit."

CHAPTER 17

Gloria gave me her worst rattletrap Ford on the theory that if I was going to get run off the road again I might as well do it in a cab already booked for demolition derby. I detoured to buy a can of pine-scented air freshener, then drove to the Zone, squealing the tight curves on Storrow Drive, beating out yellow lights down Arlington to Boylston Street.

When you pilot a Boston cab, that kind of driving is expected.

I fought the urge to stop by Sam's Charles River Park penthouse. I'd just check to see if he was home yet, I told myself. See if a female voice answered the buzzer, I told myself. Bullshit, I told myself. Who are you kidding?

I stuck a tape in my boom-box, working by feel in the dark. Bonnie Raitt strummed the first chords of "Streetlights," then the drums came in and I sang along. The mix of blues and Motown on that album soothes my Detroit native bones.

At the corner of Washington and Eliot, in the brass heart of the Zone, the weed-free lawns of Lincoln existed on some other planet. It amazes me that people from Lincoln speak the same tongue as folks who inhabit the Zone.

I speak Lincoln, but I speak Zone with a better accent, more authority. Oh, it's changed some since my cop days. The pizza shack has a fresh coat of red paint, already covered with graffiti. "Liberate El Salvador," it says over and over, interspersed with Spanish insults involving Alberto's mother and a dog. The peek-a-boo theater has new tinted window glass. Developers are eating up the vacant lots and empty buildings, encroaching fast. Some of the porno shops have fled to Saugus, Revere, Stoughton, any unsuspecting town that'll take them. The Naked I's still there, but the Pussy Cat Lounge is gone, its infamous runway sold at auction.

Every guy on the street looked like a sailor, a pimp, or an undercover cop.

When I'm in the Zone I try to see nothing but surface. I study the light bulbs that make up the signs, the mica chips in the sidewalks, the strippers' photos on the billboards.

Usually it doesn't work. That's one of the reasons I

quit being a cop. I see more than I want to, more than I can handle without turning to mush or turning to stone.

The Zone is Boston's sewer, the drain that sucks down the ones who can't quite swim. The men and women prowling the nighttime streets are mostly old hands at survival, veterans whose eyes have that time-less frozen hardness. It doesn't take the young ones long to develop the look. Children huddle in doorways, shivering and swearing, talking big. The hookers seem hungrier every year, "tough" painted on their faces along with the makeup. Hypodermic syringes float across puddles of urine. I always wonder, what hap-pened, what happened to these people?

What happened to Valerie Haslam that made her think she'd be better off here?

The lights were out in Renney's flat at the back of the alleyway. I circled the Zone's perimeter, crisscrossed the streets, loitered in spaces reserved for fire hydrants. Nobody really looks at a cab. I rescued a scared couple who'd blundered in from the theater district, ferried them to the posh Westin Hotel. They gave me a big tip, and said they hadn't realized Boston was so dirty.

I got into a routine with the cab: drive a little, wait a little, check the lights at Renney's, look under the streetlamps at the gatherings of boys and girls. Pros-titutes use the streetlamp glare to advertise the mer-chandise. The old folks, the homeless, don't care about the lights. They congregate near the heating grates.

At the end of an hour what I really wanted was a bullhorn on the top of the cab. "You!" I'd holler, my voice booming like God Almighty's, the next time some jerk cut me off with a right turn from the left-hand lane, "You, in the red Trans Am! Stupid move, asshole! Stupid move!"

Boston drivers earn their reputation. In Detroit, where I learned to drive, they had respect for automobiles.

Once I thought I saw my client, Jerry Toland, but the boy hugging the streetlamp was younger than Jerry, thinner, with brown hair. He was talking to a blonde whose skirt covered her hips but not her thighs. She kept moving those legs, marching up and down, swinging her arms against the cold. Her breath was a frosty puff of cigarette smoke.

Once I thought I saw Sam, but it was just wishful thinking, daydreaming at night. The kind of daydreaming that fogs up the windshield.

I like Sam. I like sex. I like my independence, and I don't like one-night stands. Maybe I should put an ad in the personals.

I counted the number of cop cars. I kept my eyes peeled for the gray Caprice, Mooney's hooker, Valerie Haslam. The lights in Renney's place stayed dark.

Three hours later my knee hurt, my backside was numb, I'd run out of tapes, and I was damned tired of waiting for somebody else to make a move. I screeched a corner and caught the neon flash of a Budweiser sign. It made me think about 2 A.M. closing time, and I found the cab heading, almost by itself, toward the bar where Mooney's difficulties had begun.

I parked in a loading zone, wishing I had one of those Officer on Duty cards to save me from a ticket.

Jamming my driving cap low on my forehead, I stuffed my hair underneath and grabbed my down vest off the passenger seat. It has a shapeless cut, and I didn't want anybody to think I'd mistaken the Blue Note for a dating bar. Stooping my shoulders, I went straight to the bar and sat on a vacant stool in the darkest corner of a dark room.

I needn't have bothered. At one-thirty in the morning, Dracula could perch on a bar stool in a dive like this and get served without comment. The old guy closest to me wore dirty woolen gloves with the fingers cut off. He was reading a tabloid with the headline: MIDGET TRAINS TO BE ASTRONAUT IN CLOTHES DRYER.

I ordered a Jack Daniels.

I'm not a drinker. I never acquired the taste, but I figured the bartender would be happier to talk to a whiskey drinker at three-and-a-quarter a pop than a beer guzzler at a buck-twenty-five. Not that I'd decided to question the bartender, a skinny young guy who looked wide awake, smooth, and ready to lie.

The room was maybe twenty by thirty, paneled with phony wood on the bar side. The other walls had started out yellow, but were faded to tan and splashed with water stains from leaky overhead pipes. It may have been the yellowish light, but everybody in the bar looked faded too.

Two working girls had moved chairs close to a radiator and kicked off their spikes to toast their feet against the hot metal. One wore a platinum wig; one had a punky shock of blonde hair that could have been her own. The white-haired one wore mesh stockings. The blond was flirting long distance with a lone man at a table.

Besides my tabloid reader, there were three male customers. One was a sailor, a foreigner by the oddly shaped cap. The other two were medium-sized men. Brown hair, average height, average build, nondescript in every way. Guys who'd perfected the art of hiding in plain sight.

No wonder Mooney had recalled so few witnesses.

The Jack Daniels burned the back of my throat.

A man came in with a surge of cold air and sat at a table in the back, nodding to the two hookers as he passed. He wore a lined raincoat that masked his bulk, belted without defining a waist. Something about the way he moved was familiar. I watched his reflection in the dusty mirror behind the bar. He waved at the bartender, who poured a double scotch and hustled over.

A regular.

He had dark, greasy hair, big ears, a pear-shaped face with cheeks so plump they bulged. His thin lips seemed stretched by the cheeks, fixed in a permanent, but not a friendly, grin. He wore wire-rimmed glasses.

The bartender answered my wave. I was about to slide my card on the bar and ask him where he'd been the night Mooney had a fight when the man in the raincoat yelled for another drink.

I don't forget voices. I remembered his. He was a cop.

"Beer," I said hastily, slipping my card back in my pocket. I wanted to stay undercover, too.

The bartender raised an eyebrow.

"Whatever's on draft," I said.

I couldn't recall the cop's name. I don't think our paths had crossed more than twice during my whole six-year tenure, but I'd talked to him on the phone. So he must have worked out of another division. Area D, maybe. Yeah, Area D.

The man next to me flipped the page. Princess Di Speaks to UFO Aliens, it said.

The bartender and the cop repeated the business with the double scotch, but this time there was a whispered discussion between the two men. I couldn't hear a word. I nursed my beer. It was almost closing time.

The bartender disappeared into a back room, came out with a middle-aged guy who walked with a stutter and a limp, leaning heavily on a cane. The man made his way over to where the cop sat. I watched the confrontation in the mirror.

They didn't say much, but what they said was soft and furious. Then the man in the raincoat lifted his untouched second drink and slowly, very slowly, poured it on the floor. The limping man lifted his cane like a weapon. The cop said something and the man reconsidered. The hand and the cane came down. He turned with as much dignity as he could muster and limped away. Then the cop in the raincoat headed out the door. I didn't see him pay his tab.

I laid my money on the bar and followed.

CHAPTER
18

Imitating drunks I have known, I turned right when I came out the door, hesitated, then veered left as if I couldn't make up my mind which way to go. A teenager in a T-shirt and jeans hurried by, clutching a white paper bag. I stumbled twenty paces and peered down a dismal alley. The man in the raincoat had disappeared. He must have had a car waiting nearby.

I shivered and zipped my vest against the wind. It had picked up, whirling the Styrofoam fast-food cartons down the gutter, stinging my ears. I stuck my hands in my pockets, fumbled for the car keys, and made my way back to the loading zone. No ticket. No broken windows. No dented fenders.

Was the Blue Note a regular cop watering hole? Was the guy in wire-rims keeping the place under surveillance? Did the bartender know the guy was a cop, or just that he drank Johnny Walker doubles on the rocks?

And what was this pouring-liquor-on-the-floor routine? Not the best way to stay incognito.

I decided on a few more passes. Closing time is a good time to circulate. When the bars shut down, the hookers come out.

I was letting my questions stew, driving on automatic pilot, when I saw Marla.

Marla's a regular, a lady I used to arrest maybe once every three months. She's got four kids in state care, and a drug habit that keeps her working the streets. A detox veteran, she never seems to take the cure for long. I keep hoping she'll change, but I guess she's doing the best she can.

In a red mini topped by a shiny black jacket, she must have been freezing. Her high heels were sprained-ankle specials. I have no idea of Marla's age. Her oldest kid must be fifteen.

I blocked the crosswalk and she hollered nasty things about me and my ancestors until I stuck my head out the window and waved.

"Hop in," I said.

"How come?" She is, like most hookers, suspicious.

I brandished the cash my last fare had donated.

"Who you supposed to be tonight, girl?" she said, opening the door and climbing into the passenger seat. "Turn up the heater, for Christ's sake."

The last time I saw Marla I was decked out as a sister

hooker. She could have killed my cover, but she kept quiet.

"I'm looking for somebody," I said.

"Where we going?"

"Just cruising. I'll put you down wherever you say."

"Looking for somebody," she repeated. "Down here."

"Right."

"Honey, down here is where you come not to be somebody," she said. "Ain't got no somebodies 'round here." She chuckled and nodded and I wondered what she was using to get high. I wanted to launch into a speech about AIDS and clean needles, but figured she was in no shape to pay me any mind.

"Remember Janine, with the tattoos?" I asked.

"The tattooed lady?" Marla stared out the side window. Her voice was low, the words slurred. "I think she gone away from here. Is this all the heat this junk heap puts out?"

"I saw her last night," I said.

Marla shook her head. "Lots of gals look like Janine. Seems to me I heard she got sick or something."

"Remember who you heard that from?" I asked.

"Nah."

"Remember when?"

"Nah."

I sighed and said, "How about a new one? A real young white chickie, brown hair, brown eyes, five-four?"

"She a somebody?"

"Family in Lincoln," I said.

"You ever try kicking that heater?" Marla asked.

I passed over my picture of Valerie. It was getting a

handled look to it, edges curved and worn. I flicked on the dome light so she could see it better. The streets were empty and the driving easy. Most of the boys and girls had scored for the night or given up and found shelter. There was a little action in front of the bus depot, but the bitter wind was an effective crackdown on prostitution.

Dead time, the cops used to call it.

Marla stared at the picture so long I thought she'd nodded off. Then she said, "I think I could have seen her—for what it's worth."

"If it's true, it's worth. If it's not, it's not."

"Honey, I don't tell lies to no ex-policewoman. I expect you got friends."

"A couple," I said.

"I know you ain't gonna sic 'em on me. But I do think maybe I saw this child. She wearing shoes like you wear to the senior fucking prom. White silky stuff, and I think they ain't gonna stay that color long, girl."

"Where was she?"

"Corner," Marla said. "Under some lamppost. I tell you I wasn't takin' too much note exactly where I was."

"She alone?"

"A couple gals with her. Rhonda, I think, maybe. You remember Rhonda? She talking to some dude, your girl."

"Pimp?"

"A john, maybe. White boy. Maybe a hustler. Maybe chickenhawk. Prettiest dude I ever seen. Gold hair like a picture in a church."

"When was this?" I asked.

"Dunno," she said. "Days, you know, they go on by."

"Prettiest dude I ever seen" sounded like Geoffrey Reardon to me.

"It wasn't tonight, was it?" I asked.

"I don't think so. I remember tonight okay, I think," she said.

So Reardon had lied. If it was Reardon.

"Tell me more about this guy," I said.

"Honey, I got to be going. You can let me off at the bus station, okay?"

"This guy with the blond hair," I said.

"Yeah? So what about him?"

"Seen him around?"

"Just the once. Kind of boy you remember."

We haggled a little for old times' sake, and then I gave her a twenty and dropped her at the corner of St. James. I spent the next hour holed up near my alleyway, trying to keep warm and awake. The lights never went on at Renney's. No Valerie. No Caprice. No Janine. No unnamed cop in a bulky raincoat.

On the bright side, I didn't even put a ding in the cab.

CHAPTER 19

Back home, I spent fifteen bleary-eyed minutes deciphering notes stuck under the magnets on my refrigerator door. Roz had scrawled a message from Spider telling someone, probably herself, not to miss ProtoSlime at the Rat, ProtoSlime being some rock group and the Rat being the Rathskeller in Kenmore Square, a hangout of bizarre repute. There was a note that said "peanut butter," meaning she was running out of it, and one that said "check out toilet!"

Sometimes Roz answers the phone and sometimes she doesn't, depending on her mood and hair color du jour, so I have a telephone answering machine. Its red light glowed steadily. Either Reardon hadn't gotten around to reading Valerie's diary, hadn't found anything relevant therein, or had ripped up my card as soon as he'd ushered me out his office door.

The latter possibility seemed the most likely, what with his lying about not seeing Valerie, so I tossed the place until I found the phonebook most likely to contain the address of a man who worked in Lincoln. The Metro West Directory—Ma Bell's attempt to forge an identity for Boston's western suburbs—was underneath a potted plant in my bedroom.

No Reardon, Geoffrey. I searched some more and found the Boston phonebook propping open a kitchen closet.

Reardon, Geoffrey L., lived at 228 Dudley Street, Somerville—a low-rent address. Since I have little respect for the sleep of people who lie to me, I dialed, 4 A.M. notwithstanding. I got no answer. A deep sleeper, or a man who slept away from home.

With his looks he could sleep anyplace he wanted, I thought, summoning courage to check out the second-floor bathroom. I eased open the door, saw chocolate tile, holes and pipes. A large carton rested in a corner. Peeking inside I thought I saw, yes, I did see, a perfectly appalling electric blue toilet.

Must be in transit to another bathroom, I told myself. I thought about rousing Roz. Maybe she was sleeping with someone I could question concerning the blue toilet. I decided this was not something I wanted to deal with in the wee hours and contented myself with writing a note: "Do not install this toilet!!!" and taping it to the box. Then I got undressed, unwound the Ace bandage from my knee, and pulled the covers over my head.

I dreamed about Sam Gianelli and bathtubs, bathtubs and Sam.

I don't need a lot of sleep. Not quite four hours later, I woke with the alarm, flexed my knee cautiously, and decided to try the Y. Even if I couldn't play volleyball, I could take a long hot soapy shower.

My knee loosened up as I played, and I put in a creditable game-and-a-half, once scoring three kills in a row. I don't particularly like the terminology, but there it is, and it's one of the things I do best. I'm an indifferent server, but a fine outside hitter, and outside hitters spike for a living. A kill is just a successful spike. You take a full 180-degree preparation, jump, meet the ball over the net, and smash it down and away from their blockers. If you've placed it out of diving setter range, it smacks the floor, bounces back six feet high, and is extremely satisfying.

So was the shower. I mean, it wasn't a long, luxurious bath, but compared to what I could have anticipated in my first-floor bathroom, it was great. My first-floor bathroom cannot rightly be called a bathroom, because it has no bath. It's a water closet, slightly larger than a phonebooth. The sink is wedged in a corner next to the toilet, and I have to hold my breath to get the door closed once I'm inside. The sink is one of those old-fashioned types, with separate hot and cold spigots and a rubber plug on a metal chain so that warm water can be blended in the basin. I don't have the patience for that, so I either scald myself or freeze myself whenever I use it, which is not often. I use the second-floor bath, the one that now has the holes and pipes and chocolate tile and vile blue toilet.

Maybe I could move into the Y until Twin Brothers finished the job.

I phoned Reardon's home from the Dunkin' Donuts in Central Square between bites of glazed donut and sips of strong coffee. No answer. I dialed the Emerson, getting the number from Information. A woman with a silky voice connected me to Reardon's office. The phone rang twelve times before she came back on the line and told me that Mr. Reardon was not answering. Hot news flash.

In between the time she'd disappeared and the time I'd questioned him, someone who looked like Reardon had visited someone who looked like Valerie in the Zone. I have what Mooney always called an "overactive imagination," so I could come up with any number of explanations, ranging from the bizarre—Reardon running a chain of high-priced prep-school hookers—to the ridiculous—Reardon discovering one of his students by chance while cruising for a lady of the night. Somehow I couldn't see gorgeous Geoffrey paying for sex. None of my explanations had the nice simple ring of probable truth.

I headed down Route 2 to the Emerson, one eye on the speedometer, the other seeking traffic cops, hoping Reardon could dish up a story I'd believe. It was a good day for a little speed, brisk and bright, and once I crested the hill into Lexington I surrendered to the impulse. Someday, a sports car.

I parked under my cherry tree and headed through the main gate and across the quadrangle to Reardon's office. A bunch of teenage boys kicked a soccer ball on the muddy field. One of the tame squirrels crossed my path and flew up a tree. It was as big as a cat. Not as big as T.C., but then he's tall for his age.

A four-by-six card was taped to Reardon's office door. It said: "Classes canceled for the day." It was signed with a flourish: "Geoffrey L. Reardon."

I lurked in the hallway, casually reading a bulletin board, until two girls finished wailing over a homework assignment and disappeared. I tried the door. Locked.

A credit card will do the trick nine times out of ten. The tenth time you'll split the card, and it's such a pain to explain that you need a new VISA because the old one failed while breaking and entering. So I carry what is known in the trade as a "loid," a thin strip of celluloid that slips down between the door and the jamb and snicks those lousy little bolts back before you can dial 911. I was in Reardon's office as quickly as if I'd had a key.

The drawer that had been filled with notebooks was empty. I sank into Reardon's desk chair and dialed his home number. Seven rings. Eight. I yanked his center drawer open while I waited. Pencils, erasers, scissors, tape—the same stuff I'd pawed through two days ago.

I sat up straight. Someone had taken the phone off the hook.

"Hello," I said cautiously.

Someone grunted.

"Hello," I repeated. "Mr. Reardon?"

"Yeah? What?"

"Mr. Reardon?" I repeated.

"Which one?" The voice was gruff, male.

"Geoffrey."

"Not here."

"Don't hang up. Please, it's important. Do you know where he is?"

"Lady, I'm half asleep. He's not here. He's at work."

"I'm calling from the Emerson. He's not here."

"He must be. The Reliant's gone."

It took me a minute to realize he meant a car.

"'Bye," said the voice on the phone. Then I heard a click and then nothing but a hum.

Damn. The car was gone. The man was gone. The diary was gone. Valerie was gone.

I searched the desk again, to make sure he hadn't transferred his paperwork from drawer to drawer. The key was still under the blotter. As I fitted it into the bottom-drawer keyhole, my fingers felt a roughness and I leaned closer for a better look. There were scratches, scratches I hadn't left there. Strictly amateur hairpin stuff.

The bottle of Wild Turkey had been shoved to the back to make room for a pile of diaries, maybe twenty in all. I leafed through them quickly. Most had a name inscribed on the front. Two had the name scrawled in the upper left-hand corner of the inside cover. None of the names was Valerie's. I went through the pile again, making sure one book hadn't been tucked inside another by mistake.

Then I gazed longingly at the bottle of Wild Turkey, which proves how upset I was. Wild Turkey at ten-thirty in the morning. Ugh.

I had the strong feeling that Reardon and Valerie were in a Plymouth Reliant motoring toward some southern state where you could marry your first cousin provided you were both over the age of eight.

I pitched the diaries back in the drawer, relocked it,

and went out into the hallway. I wondered if Reardon had put up the sign yesterday or this morning. Maybe I'd missed him by minutes.

The doorway to the little theater was closed, but unlocked. Backstage, it was pitch black. When I opened the door something stirred, so I reached in my purse and yanked out a can of hair spray that fooled me by its shape. I use that old-fashioned lacquer-style hair spray as a substitute for Mace. It costs less and is just as effective. I tried again and got my flashlight. I ran it around the stage perimeter and heard the scrambles and giggles of teenagers getting dressed in the dark. Puppy love. Puppy sex.

"Reardon?" I called into the sudden hush.

"He's not here," said a boy whose voice threatened to squeak.

"You see him today?" I asked.

"No." This voice was female, childish.

"Thanks," I said. I turned off the flash and left the room to young love.

My knee was starting to stiffen again, so I decided on the long way back to the car, thinking a walk might do it—and me—good. The long way led past a rustic shack, built to look older than it was and hold gardeners' tools or maybe athletic equipment without ruining the tone of the place. The path wound through stands of pine trees, oaks just beginning to bud. The sun shone brightly and even I, a woman nervous out of sight of concrete, began to enjoy my country ramble.

Right before making a sharp left to get back to the car, I turned for a final view of the school buildings, the athletic fields, the trees, the squirrels—and I stopped dead and waited.

What's wrong with this picture?

That was my first conscious thought, that something was wrong.

Later I realized it was the wheel tracks cut into the sod where no vehicle should have gone, coupled with the steady drone of an automobile engine. Now, in no hurry, merely curious, I followed the tracks over a rise, past stately pines.

The car was a black Plymouth Reliant, maybe five years old. The engine was running and a corrugated vacuum cleaner hose snaked from the tail pipe through the right rear window.

Someone was inside, slumped over, head resting on the driver's window. I ran the last fifty yards, forgetting my knee.

I grabbed the front-door handle. Locked. All the doors were locked. Bright gold hair pressed against the glass. Given time and tools, I can crack a car.

I shouted. The hair didn't move. I pounded the glass. The hair didn't move.

I ran around and yanked the hose from the back window, shoving it behind the car so it would spill its poison far from me. There was maybe a two-inch gap at the top of the window. I shoved my hand in, choking from the fumes, then pulled away and stripped off my gloves, my jacket, rolled up the sleeve of my shirt, anything to make my arm thinner, make it slip down far enough to pull up the button, open the door.

I could make it through to about six, seven inches above my wrist. The button was three inches away. It might as well have been a mile.

What do you use to break a car window—a shoe? a

rock? I was wearing sneakers. There were only pebbles on the ground. I remembered the feel of the flashlight in my hand, and I grabbed it out of my bag.

It was safety glass; it wouldn't shatter, I reminded myself. I could stand close without getting cut. The first time I hit it, it just cracked, so I wound up, the way I do for a volleyball spike, and drove the flashlight damn near through the glass. Then I used my coat to shield my hand, reached through, and unlocked the passenger door.

It opened easily. I kneeled on the front seat, grabbed Reardon's shoulders, and started hauling him out of the car. He was unwieldy, the way drunks are, lolling and heavy. His left foot stuck behind the gear shift and I had to crawl into the back seat, reach over, and free it. I knew he was dead before I got him onto the grass. Still I held my fingers to the pulse at his throat. He was cold.

A stiff. That's what we used to call them when I was a cop. We never gave them the dignity of a first name, a last name. A stiff is not a human being. A stiff is nobody's mother, nobody's child, nobody's teacher, nobody's friend. A stiff made the job possible.

Sometimes we named them for their choice of death—floater, croaker, roast.

I looked away from Geoffrey Reardon's face, away from the half-open blue eyes, the spill of golden hair, and turned him into a stiff so I could go on with my job.

I pulled my right glove on, reached into the car, and shut off the motor, leaving the keys in the ignition. There was a notebook on the seat. I grabbed it, thinking it was Valerie's missing diary. It was the manuscript of Reardon's play. I riffled the pages. Nothing fell out. I checked the rest of the car, the glove compartment, the cassette holder. I felt under the seats. Old Kleenex and loose change.

Twenty feet away, I sat on the ground and made myself breathe, in and out, in and out. Deeper and slower. Then I walked back to Reardon's office, 'loided the lock again, and carefully wiped my prints off the doorknobs, the desk, and the phone.

I tried to remember if I knew anybody in the Lincoln Police Department, but I couldn't come up with a name. I left Reardon's office, went to the building closest to Reardon's body, the one to which I'd have logically fled after finding the grim scene in the woods. I asked a gray-haired woman where I could find a phone. Student lounge, she said, pointing straight ahead. The place with the blue velvet couches. I wanted to sink into one of them and sleep for a week.

I punched 911. The bored voice perked up and turned officious when I mentioned the Emerson School. I gave my name and told the voice I'd meet the patrolmen at the scene. Then I found a dime and called home, reaching my own message machine which was what I wanted. Maybe Reardon had phoned after I'd left.

Holding my remote beeper to the receiver, I pressed the button. It made a noise like a turkey gobbling.

There was the scratchy sound of tape, then Mooney's voice. He said: "Hey, I'm going into this hearing pretty damn soon. You got anything? Do I owe you or do you owe me?"

Then there was a beep and a second message.

"Hello. This is Preston Haslam. Valerie's come home, safe and sound. Please send me a bill for your time, and thanks for your concern."

CHAPTER
20

The Lincoln Police, repre-
sented by an aging lieu-
tenant and a patrolman too young to shave, gawked,
poked, and nodded, murmuring "roger" and "over and
out" into their walkie-talkies while shooting sidelong
glances to see if I was trying to eavesdrop. They seemed
united by one desire: to avoid calling in the State Police.
If it was homicide, what with all the petty larcencies
and minor drug deals already on their plate, they'd
need to holler for the Staties. Therefore Geoffrey Reardon had committed suicide. Open and shut.

I was the sole fly buzzing the ointment. If a private
cop hadn't been around, I don't think they'd have

raised a sweat, just called the meat wagon and written the report. I could practically see the thought balloons over the head of the young one: "Drama teacher kills himself. Well, why the hell not? Probably a faggot. Maybe had AIDS, for Christ's sake."

The rookie, pursing his lips and looking like he wanted to rush to the patrol car for a pair of rubber gloves, used the tips of two fingers to extract Reardon's wallet from his pants pocket.

I'd wondered about Reardon's sexual preference myself. He'd given off conflicting signals. His incredible beauty and the signed photo of the gorgeous guy in his desk drawer pointed one way. His flirtatious manner and his photo collection of scantily clad teenage girls led another.

Now that the adrenaline had quit on me, I could feel the cold in my toes and my knee. I kept rubbing the tip of my nose and thinking about frostbite.

The Emerson had clout. No doubt about it. The cops made a silent approach—no flashing lights or tacky stuff like that. Refraining from blocking campus roads, they maintained a deferential attitude to a Mrs. Filicia Stoner, Vice Principal in Charge of Damage Control, who must have gotten a phone call as soon as I reported Reardon's death. Mrs. Stoner had been loosed to deal with the matter diplomatically, and it was fun to watch a pro at work.

A dignified woman with a graying bun, she viewed the corpse, said, "He must have been deeply unhappy, poor man," with just the right tone of pained regret. She declared she knew she could trust Lieutenant Harrison to handle every little detail. As to next-of-kin, she would inform Mr. Reardon's brother—she believed it was a brother—whose name and address were surely in Mr. Reardon's personnel file. If, of course, that was all right with the officer in charge?

Harrison, the older cop, beamed.

Then she turned her gaze on me. "And you are here with the police," she said.

It wasn't really a question and it wasn't really a statement. I got the feeling she expected me to wither under her stare and confess to responsibility for Reardon's death. Or at least for the awful circumstance of his death occurring on hallowed Emerson ground.

Harrison jerked his chin in my direction. "Private investigator," he said. "Came to talk to Reardon. Found the body."

"I don't believe we met when you checked in at the office," Ms. Stoner said.

"I don't believe we did," I replied with my best smile.

"If Mr. Reardon had private business with you, we would, of course, expect him to conduct that business on his own time," she recited.

"Of course," I agreed, politely not pointing out that time and Reardon no longer kept company.

She waited for me to elaborate and when I didn't she said, "I would appreciate it if you'd drop by my office on your way out." Her voice, warm when it flattered the cop, acquired an edge of frost.

I could tell by her steely eye that the amount of information I could squeeze out of Ms. Stoner wasn't worth the trip.

"Nice meeting you," I said.

She did a pivot the nuns must have taught her at school—straight-shouldered, tight-hipped—and snubbed me in dignified silence.

Since the mighty Ms. Stoner had given them the okay to be rude, the cops weren't concentrating on charm when they questioned me. So I left out the part about searching Reardon's office. They wanted to see how the hose had been stuffed in the crack of the window and I showed them as best I could, given the shards of glass.

And what was I doing at the Emerson anyway?

I bit back my automatic "free country" response.

I said I'd had an appointment to speak to Reardon concerning a runaway student. On my way, I'd noticed the tire tracks, heard the engine, come down to investigate.

Ah ha! Then how did I know the identity of the victim? Gotcha!

Sorry, boys, but I'd seen the man before—yesterday. Wanted to ask him a few follow-up questions.

Who's the runaway student?

Really, I didn't see where that was any of their business, I said, not being dumb enough to speculate about the affairs of a client—or an ex-client—in front of two cops.

They wanted to know if Reardon had seemed depressed when I spoke to him yesterday.

Not noticeably.

Had he said anything odd, anything that might cast some light on subsequent events?

I liked that "subsequent events." It's standard cop-report-speak. I told them he'd mentioned leaving his teaching job.

Ahhhhh. That was the kind of bilge they wanted to hear. They made it sound like a suicide note. They really wanted a suicide note. They thought somebody ought to read the guy's play. Maybe, the old cop thought, it was, like, this super-long suicide note. Each of them thought the other guy ought to read it.

I stuffed my hands in my pockets and tried to think about warm days on Cape beaches. It didn't work.

I had a friend who killed himself. End of October, eight years ago. He didn't leave a note either. For a long time I used to see him—imagine I'd seen him—in a group of people waiting for a bus, or driving by in a strange new car. I still scream at him in my dreams, incoherent pleas to stop. Talk to me. Let me help.

My ex-husband's trying to kill himself—slowly, with cocaine. He says it helps his music. I say it helps him deal with the fact that his music doesn't get the attention he thinks it deserves, but then I'm a cold bitch or so he said when we split.

According to my mom my grandmother always used to say: *A mensh zol lebn nor fun naygerikeyt vegn*, which, translated from the Yiddish, means: "A person should live, if only for curiosity's sake" and sums up my thoughts on suicide pretty well.

Neither my ex nor my friend would see a shrink, God forbid. That might be admitting something was wrong. It seems to me killing yourself is one hell of a way to admit something's wrong.

Nobody's ever accused me of being a Pollyanna, but I mean, what if the damn thing could be fixed?

Face it, I have trouble with suicide. I think to myself, okay, you're dying of a fatal disease and it's painful as hell—well, maybe. Maybe if I couldn't move and I couldn't see and I hurt all the time . . . but don't turn off the damn machine if I can still hear music. Put on some fine wailing blues. Hit me with Willie Brown or Mississippi John Hurt and I might surprise you yet.

Geoffrey Reardon's death looked like suicide, smelled like suicide, tasted like suicide. And maybe what I was refusing to believe was that a man could be in that much pain—physical, psychic, whatever—and I could spend half an hour talking to him and never get a hint. But then I never got a hint with my friend.

What the hell do I know about people? Even the ones I think I know.

On the phone Preston Haslam sounded delighted that his little girl was home again. He didn't react one way or another to the news about Reardon's death, except to say he hoped it wouldn't upset Valerie. Jerry Toland sounded troubled, but thought my work was done.

I hesitated about sending a bill. That's unusual. Normally I send them quick and they pay them slow. So something must have seemed wrong before I realized it was wrong.

I waited for the autopsy report. I wrote Paolina a long letter. I played a lot of guitar, toughening the calluses on my fingers. And I buried myself in my other case.

Mooney's hearing was speedily approaching and as far as I knew nobody but me had laid eyes on Janine. Joanne hadn't returned my calls about the license plate. Sunday, I dialed her from the phone in the kitchen while finishing off a late lunch I'd culled from foil-wrapped bundles of suspicious leftovers. Busy signal. Always busy or take a message or nothing. You'd think the whole damn police department had moved out of town.

A thud from upstairs made me jump. Twin Brothers at work. I mean, I should be used to it by now, right? I took a deep breath and climbed the stairs.

I'm glad to report that the weird blue toilet had disappeared, replaced by a quite respectable tan number the Twin Bros informed me was "almond," in tones that let me know I had proved my hitherto only suspected total ignorance of the plumbing world. The Day-Glo orange sink had come back and I could hardly wait to see what they'd hook up in the way of a tub.

Roz and the guys were all in the bathroom, which made my entrance almost impossible.

"I thought the tile was out," I said. They seemed to be busily gluing the chocolate stuff in place.

"This tile is terrific," Roz said. She was wearing a deep blue T-shirt with scarlet letters on the front: "Time flies like an arrow." On the back it said: "Fruit flies like a banana." It's tough to argue with someone wearing a truly stupid shirt.

"I hate it," I said.

"You can't get the full effect until it's done, Carlotta."

"I don't want the full effect."

"Look," Roz drew me aside, no mean feat in the four-by-ten environs, "with the dark tile, the tub and the toilet and the sink, they're, like, gonna be floating in the room. Wait till you see the mural on the ceiling."

"Mural?"

"Like a fresco, you know. Like the Sistine Chapel."

"Make no mistake, Roz. This is not the Sistine Chapel."

"Well, what about a desert scene on the tile around the bathtub?" she said earnestly. "I mean, wouldn't it be great to be in the middle of this desert and, like, sopping wet?"

I had choices. I could strangle Roz. I could make her move out immediately and find somebody else to clean my house. I could fire the Twin Bros. and hire other incompetents to finish my bathroom. I could stop clenching my jaw before my teeth broke.

The doorbell rang while I was simmering. Roz looked relieved.

"Later," I said menacingly.

"Later," she agreed.

"No desert scene," I said.

The bell rang again. I clattered downstairs and stuck my right eye to the peephole. I always check.

Even with the distortion I recognized the face. The man was blond, square-jawed, blue-eyed. He was the original of the "movie star" photo I'd admired in Geoffrey Reardon's desk.

CHAPTER
21

Maybe if he'd been ugly I'd have had my shoulder to the door where it belonged. He barged past me into the hall, stopped after three long paces, and pivoted slowly, staring at my foyer like it was someplace he wanted to remember, and believe me, the decor is not great—just the old oak coatstand in the corner and a few of Roz's less weird acrylics on the walls. One, a close-up study of a garlic bulb, is certainly worth a second glance. You look at it too long, it practically starts to smell.

She wants me to replace it with one of her newer works featuring Smurfs and condoms in various combinations. She says they have a strong social message. Not in my foyer, I told her. Strangers come to my door. Jehovah's Witnesses. Fuller Brush Men. Clients.

As the guy studied my foyer, I sized him up, and it was a pleasure. I'm partial to dark-haired men, but I have nothing against slim blonds with bony faces and deep-set eyes.

Blue eyes. He turned them on me with startling suddenness, like a bird of prey eyeing breakfast.

"This you?" he demanded, brandishing what looked like a business card.

I closed the door and leaned against it. "The print is small," I said. The guy was gorgeous but I didn't care much for his manners. He was wearing pleated-front wool pants and a leather bomber jacket. He wasn't holding a notebook, but I hoped he'd brought Valerie's diary, maybe zipped in the front of his jacket. Reardon had probably left it for me somewhere, at his house or . . .

Without so much as an invitation, the guy sped into the living room. When I followed, he was giving the place the once over, practically memorizing it like he'd done the hall.

"Can I help you?" I asked in a pretty hostile tone.

"This." He raised the card again. "Is it yours?"

"I can't see it," I said.

"Sorry." He held it maybe three inches closer. Great. Now I could tell it had print on it.

"Why don't you read it to me?" I said.

"Why don't you come over and take a closer look," he said with a smile. Again his appearance got in my way. If he'd had the face of a gerbil I would have been more cautious, more wary. As it was, he held the card out, I marched over, and the next thing I knew, I felt a knife blade at my neck.

"Don't scream," he said quietly.

I would have nodded my agreement but I didn't want the blade to nick me.

"Why?" the guy said. "Just tell me why?"

I probably said something like "huh," something brilliant. The world had frozen. The room seemed the same. Aunt Bea's oriental rug glowed in the sunlight. I noticed how worn the beige sofa looked near the edge of the wooden scrollwork. The rocker sat balanced, motionless. The only noise came from Red Emma scuffling around in the gravel at the bottom of her cage. It was almost as loud as my breathing.

"Why did you have to do it?" he insisted.

"What?" I managed, my mouth dry, my lips moving as little as possible.

"Why couldn't you leave him alone? He wasn't hurting anybody."

Roz was upstairs. The Twin Brothers were upstairs. All within call, if I could call. Roz knows karate. I don't. I'm a street fighter, police academy–trained.

The guy maneuvered himself behind me and to my left. He was a lefty, gripping the knife in his left hand. It was jerking around more than it should have. The point rasped my collarbone, slid up. It took me a while to realize that the movement was unintentional, pure nervousness on my assailant's part. That may have been because I was nervous myself. The guy's right hand clasped my right shoulder. He was breathing hard and shallow.

"Maybe I'd better look at that card," I said softly. I

didn't like the positioning. I thought I could take the jerk. He was my height, thin. He didn't look like a fighter. He looked like a model, decorative. His grip on my shoulder was hesitant. He didn't do this sort of thing for a living.

I wished I'd worn a different bra, not the one with the safety pin holding the shoulder strap together. My mother always warned me: Wear torn underwear and you'll be embarrassed when they take you to the hospital.

"Geoff told me about you," he whispered in my ear.

"Look," I said, keeping my voice low and even with effort, "you are making one hell of a mistake. I'd like to explain it to you—"

"Go ahead," he said angrily. "Explain."

"Yeah," I said, "I'd love to. But I don't talk real well with a knife at my throat." I increased my volume on the last bit, hoping Roz might be at the foot of the stairs by now.

His hand was shaking. I couldn't feel the tip of the knife point any more. I strained my eyes trying to see where it was. My nose got in the way. I couldn't see his face, but his grasp on my shoulder loosened a bit, and he was making some kind of guttural noise deep in his throat that might have been crying. I probably could have talked him out of the knife, but I was angry now. I get angry when assholes put knives near my arteries. So I slammed my elbow back as hard as I could into his ribs, bringing my neck down tight to my chest at the same time for protection. I reached over my right shoulder with my right arm, grabbed a fistful of hair, ducked, and yanked with everything I had. He flipped over my shoulder and smacked resoundingly into Aunt Bea's rocking chair. The knife skittered across the floor. I dove for it. It was a little bastard, no more than a three-inch blade. I snapped it shut, pocketed it, crossed the room to my desk, and grabbed my .38 out of the drawer.

The effect was ruined by the fact that I keep the damn thing wrapped up and unloaded and everything. Safety first. Luckily, my friend on the floor stayed down for the count. I doubt it would have made the right impression if he'd seen me unwinding the gun from its undershirt. I didn't have time for bullets.

He groaned, then rolled onto one shoulder and took his weight on his arm with a deeper groan, more surprised than wounded, by the look of it. He stared at the room again, taking inventory. Then he shook his head gently, side to side, and looked like he was trying to wake from a bad dream.

"You can get up now," I said, pointing the empty gun.

Roz chose that moment to trip downstairs. "Everything all right?" she chirped. "I heard a noise."

"Time flies like a banana," I said. "If I need you, I'll holler."

"Okay," she said, taking in the guy on the floor, the gun, the overturned furniture, and disappearing back up the stairs. Roz has no curiosity.

"Get up," I said to handsome.

He did.

"Put your stupid card on the chair, the one you want me to read so much."

He did.

"Now back away from it and sit on the couch. Keep your hands on your thighs and move real slowly, okay?"

The card was one of mine. He hadn't attacked the wrong woman. I tossed it on the floor, but it made no satisfactory noise.

"What the fuck is this about, you moron?" I yelled, providing the sound effects myself. I'm not proud of it, or of the fact that I knocked over the desk chair for emphasis. I don't swear much anymore. I used to curse with the best of them when I was on the force, and maybe having a gun in my hand again put the words in my mouth. Maybe it was that I was so goddamned angry I could barely see. I hate the idea, the very idea, that some jerk with a knife could get behind me in my own house. I hate the idea that I could get killed and spend my last moments bleeding on Aunt Bea's rug, wondering why the hell I was dying.

"I wasn't going to hurt you," he said.

My eyebrows rose. "Good time to tell me," I said.

"I mean it," he said, as if it mattered.

"Really," I said, letting the sarcasm drip.

"Really," he echoed.

"Damn straight you weren't going to hurt me, you total jackass!" I said. "You moron! You ever hold a knife before?"

"Not that way," he said softly. "I can't believe I did it. I can't believe it. I don't know—"

He kept shaking his head gently from side to side. He had a red mark on his temple that was going to make quite a spectacular bruise. Goddamn amateurs. They can cut your throat by mistake.

"So." I picked up the chair and settled it on the floor,

keeping the gun aimed at the part in his blond hair. "If you weren't going to hurt me," I asked, "just what the hell kind of charade are you playing?"

The man bowed his head and stared at the floor as if he were looking at something else, something gruesome and terrible. I hoped he wasn't going to throw up.

I put the gun down on the desktop, well within grabbing range although I didn't think he was going to give me any more grief, and sat down. My knee felt funny. Both knees, actually.

I sucked in a deep breath and raised my hand to my neck. There was a scratch, so faint and fine I could barely feel it. No blood.

"So who the hell are you?" I said to the guy. He hadn't moved a muscle, except for one at the corner of his mouth that was twitching on its own accord. "Oh yeah, Reardon kept your photo in his desk drawer. You must be a friend."

The guy looked up at me. "And what's that supposed to mean?" he said.

"Look," I said, "let's not get all sensitive. I don't care what kind of relationship you and Reardon shared—"

"We were *brothers*," he said. "I'm Stuart Reardon."

"Shit," I murmured. The one Ms. Stoner had marched off to notify.

He said, "You assumed a little different, right? Just because Geoff was—"

"I'm sorry," I said. The two men were superficially similar, same height, same coloring. I wouldn't have picked them as brothers.

He waited a while, then said, "*Sorry*. Is that all you are? *Sorry?*"

"What am I supposed to say? In this little script in your head?"

There was a sudden burst of pounding from upstairs. Stuart shook his head and murmured, "I never even thought there'd be somebody else in the house. I never even thought about it."

He kept mumbling to himself. Amateurs.

"You make a great criminal mastermind," I said. "Go ahead. Talk."

"You don't seem to get it, do you?" he said. He tapped his chest with his left hand. "I know. I know you went to see him. And then . . . he killed himself." He whispered the last three words as if they were too awful to say out loud.

"I visit a lot of people, and believe me, not all of them expire."

"You were hired to screw things up for him at the Emerson. I mean, it wasn't bad enough he was hounded out of Wellfleet. I want to know who you were working for. Just tell me that."

"And you'll go stick your knife in them? Sure."

"I'll find out."

"Look," I said, "I'll make it easy. I never worked for anybody from Wellfleet. I don't even know anybody in Wellfleet. I don't know anything about Reardon's juicy past, although I admit you intrigue me. I went to see him because one of his students ran away. That's it."

Stuart shook his head some more, trying to clear the fog. He opened and closed his eyes. Next, I thought, he'll pinch himself.

Very slowly, he said, "And Geoff knew that? He knew you just wanted to talk about some stupid runaway?"

"Yep," I said. "I left my card on his desk. Then we talked the next day."

"I don't believe you," he said.

"You want a drink?" I asked.

"Yeah."

"You got any more knives you're gonna pull if I leave you for half a minute?"

He shook his head, and I believed him. I believed him, but I stuck the gun in the waistband of my jeans before heading for the kitchen. I figured if I left it lying on the desk, he'd guess it wasn't loaded. Maybe not. He looked shell-shocked.

I probably looked worse.

I don't keep much in the way of whiskey, but Roz likes her scotch so I poured a lot into a glass, hurried back to the living room, and gave it to him. He downed it like club soda. I had a gulp myself, straight from the bottle. It burned all the way down.

"Why don't we start over," I said, back in the desk chair.

"Okay."

"You're Reardon's brother," I said.

"I'm a tech writer at Digital," he said. For a minute I thought he was going to stick out his hand so I could shake it, but he thought better of it, and stared at the floor.

Fooled by appearances again. I'd assumed he was the male model type, not a respectable computer company employee.

"Geoff was my only family," he continued, glancing at his empty glass with regret. I refilled it from the bottle I'd placed strategically on the desk. "I mean," he continued, "we weren't always that close, but lately, it's been better. He was there for me and I was there for him, you know? And now—oh, shit."

His outburst prompted the parakeet to one of her infrequent speech attacks. "Oh, shit," she squawked. "I'm a pretty bird. Fluffy's a pretty bird." She hasn't got her name straight, but at least her vocabulary is getting spicier. Just as I decided to lower the cover on her cage, lest I get a fit of inappropriate giggles, she subsided. She can tell when I've had enough.

I turned my attention back to my blond friend. "So let me get this right. You thought you knew why your brother killed himself."

"It was the only thing that made any sense."

"See if it makes sense to me," I said.

"Geoff's a teacher. He's been a teacher—God knows—forever. He shouldn't have been. He should have been rich, you know? So he could have been a playwright, a full-time playwright, maybe a screenwriter. It's tricky, being a high school teacher, being gay. Bi, really. I mean, I know some people say there isn't any such thing as a true bisexual, but Geoff was damn close. He used to tell me it was perfectly okay for the big husky male teachers to hit on the little twelve-year-old girls. That's fine. That's 'normal,' but Geoff—well, he always had to be on the defensive."

"This is the eighties, right?" I said.

"Yeah. That makes it worse. AIDS. The paranoia is incredible."

I nodded.

"Could I have a glass of water?" he asked. "If I keep on drinking this stuff—"

"Yeah," I said, "you might do something crazy."

He actually blushed, and I did the routine with the kitchen and the gun again.

After he drank some water, which comes out of my tap an interesting yellowish shade, his voice was stronger.

"Six years ago," he said, "maybe seven, Geoff got arrested on the Cape, in Wellfleet, at some kind of trumped-up raid on a gay bar. He was never convicted. The whole thing was just designed to throw a scare into the bar owner, to make him move out. Geoff was teaching at a school in the same town, and they fired him. It's in the contract: 'Moral Turpitude.' Geoff didn't fight it. I mean, he could have, because it was just an arrest, not a conviction, and 'Moral Turpitude' is not exactly a clear legal concept. He did hire a lawyer and the lawyer hammered out this agreement with the school board, that they couldn't talk about his arrest, couldn't mention it. I mean, they didn't give Geoff a recommendation, but they let him resign. It was a technicality, but it meant he could still teach, still earn a living."

"I understand," I said.

"He was a damn good teacher. He'd never touch a student. He wouldn't dream of touching a student. Sometimes if a kid was gay, and he asked, Geoff would tell him, just tell the poor kid he wasn't the only gay person in the world, because it gave the poor kid some hope, you know, that there was somebody else like him, somebody who was making it. Outsiders pay a high price at the Emerson. Everybody's got to be cut from the same cookie cutter. Geoff was different. He was a wonderful person, and a fine writer. He shouldn't have had to work so hard."

Stuart drank the rest of his water. I waited.

He said, "I thought you'd gone there to tell him his teaching career was kaput. I thought some wacko on that school board had decided to wreak vengeance on homosexuals and tell the Emerson all. And that Geoff couldn't face starting over again, with no seniority, no nothing . . ."

"That wasn't it," I said.

He sat there for about three minutes with his face working. Then he said. "I don't understand."

"You're telling me he had no reason to kill himself," I said.

"I could make sense out of it if he was gonna be fired. I mean, not really sense, but—"

"He wasn't sick?" I said.

"No. Absolutely not."

"Depressed?"

"Hell, no. When Geoff was down, he danced. The adrenaline picked him up. He worked. He wrote. He had friends."

"Did he talk to you about quitting his job?" I asked.

"No. Never. He liked it there."

"What about getting his play produced? Did he say anything about that?"

"What the hell are you talking about?"

"And when was the last time you talked to him?"

"Maybe three weeks ago. We had dinner sometimes. Our apartments are real close, and like, Thursday night, I just stayed at his place. I've got a key."

"When did you get to his apartment?"

"Real late. Practically Friday morning. I've been working crazy overtime, and I thought we'd have breakfast together."

"I'm the one who called asking for him."

"Did I answer?"

"Yeah. You told me he was at the Emerson."

"I don't remember."

"But you weren't worried when he didn't come home."

"Nah. I figured he was staying with somebody."

"He had a lover."

"Usually. Nobody regular. I mean, with Geoff you couldn't even hazard a guess—male or female. He got off on beautiful people."

"What about a student?" I asked.

"No," he said. "I don't think so."

"Did he ever mention a girl named Valerie?"

"I don't think oo. I don't know."

I wondered where Valerie had been the day Geoff Reardon died.

Stuart pushed his hair back off his forehead, grimacing at the pain in his shoulder. Then he said, "This is going to sound dumb."

"Be my guest," I said.

"You investigate things, right?"

I held out my business card. "Right."

"Can I hire you to investigate Geoff's . . . this?"

"You mean if I decide not to turn you in for attempted murder?"

"Yeah," he said.

"I ought to," I said. "it was incredibly dumb, as stunts go. I could have killed you. You could have fallen on the stupid knife."

"I'm sorry," he said. "I'm really sorry."

"'Sorry' doesn't stitch wounds," I said. My mother used to say something like that. "Sorry doesn't fix a broken vase," I think it was.

"Yeah," he said, fingering his temple. "Shit. I can't do anything right. You might as well turn me in. I can't believe it. I can't believe Geoff killed himself, but I can't believe he was murdered or something. Maybe I should talk to the cops."

"Maybe you should hire me," I said.

"Huh?"

"That's what you were asking, wasn't it?"

"Hire you to investigate a . . . murder?"

"Look, the Lincoln cops don't think it's murder, and I don't think it would do you any good to mention the possibility. If it's murder, I'm out of it. A private cop can't meddle in that kind of stuff in this state. But if it's not murder, I might be able to help you. I could find out what your brother had on his mind. I could check if he'd had any heavy financial losses. Find out if he was seeing a shrink. That kind of stuff."

"Is it expensive? I mean, I've got the funeral to take care of—"

"Look, I'm interested in this case from another angle," I said. "That brings my fees way down. And you might be able to help with something. That brings 'em down even lower."

He said, "Oh, yeah?"

"Your brother had a drawerful of class diaries in his desk a few days ago. I'd like to see them. One of them, anyway."

"Diaries? In his desk at work?"

"Notebooks his drama class kept, the class he called the misfits."

"You want me to get them?"

"They're not at his office now, not the one I want anyway. It could be at his apartment."

"I can't go back there. Not yet. Really. I'm sorry."

I took one of my contract forms out of the top drawer of the desk. "But you have a key, right?" I said. "And if you sign one of these, give me a buck for a retainer, and lend me the key—I can."

CHAPTER
22

The mailman came up my front walk as Stuart Reardon, holding his wadded handkerchief against his temple, staggered down. I hadn't offered my assailant any cold towels or ice cubes. As a matter of fact, I hoped his head hurt like hell.

T.C. got bills, circulars, a copy of *Mother Jones*, and a sales pitch from a Hong Kong tailor who didn't carry his size. I was about to dump the whole lot in the waste basket when I noticed the Colombian stamp.

I slit the envelope with Reardon's knife.

Dear Carlotta—

She'd used regulation airmail stationery and drawn faint lines to help keep the letters straight.

I skimmed it to see if she said when she'd be back.

Dear Carlotta—
   How are you? I want to come home. Have you ever heard of a man named Carlos Roldan Gonzales? My mother and the man they say is my grandfather fight all day.
   I hate it here. I'm going to run away. Maybe I can stow away on a boat and come back to you.

Love ya,
Paolina

Terrific, I thought. Another runaway. I stuck Reardon's knife in my top drawer, thinking how upset and angry Paolina would be if I let some jerk kill me while she was away. She was always scared something would happen to me while I was a cop.

I wondered why Marta was fighting with her father. And who Carlos Roldan Gonzales was, and what the "man they say is my grandfather" business was all about. Since Bogota isn't a seaport, I wasn't too worried about boats and stowaways. But I was worried about Paolina.

I've never been to Bogota, so my image is warped by news accounts of kidnappings and drug wars. I remembered a Channel 5 special report featuring gangs of hungry beggar children, and I prayed Marta would keep a sharp eye on her daughter.

Her daughter. I'd almost thought *my* daughter, but Paolina wasn't mine.

I took her letter into the kitchen. It wasn't dinnertime by a long shot, but hunger gnawed. Getting almost stabbed had something to do with it. Every time I've stared down a gun barrel or hit the floor under fire, I've gotten incredibly ravenous, or felt terribly sexy, or both.

Considering the state of my social life, I was glad I was only hungry. I had a sudden vision of Sam and how great he'd looked at the garage. I focused on food.

I stood on tiptoe and reached way in the back of the tiny cupboard over the refrigerator for my secret shrinking hoard of TV Time popcorn. Roz thinks I hide dope there. TV Time is great popcorn, but damned if the manufacturers haven't joined the microwave revolution. When my stash runs out, I'm going to have to buy a microwave just so I can make decent popcorn.

There's progress for you.

I shook the stuff in a battered four-quart pot over an old-fashioned gas flame, feeling righteous. None of this stick-the-bag-in-the-oven-and-wait laziness for me. I melted too much butter, got a Pepsi out of the fridge, and figured I'd skip dinner.

Red Emma joined me at the kitchen table. She adores popcorn, practically inhales it. Then she has coughing fits because she gets salted out, and I have to feed her about a gallon of water.

"So," I said to her, "think he'd have knifed me, with you there as a witness and all?"

"Fluffy is a pretty bird," she said.

I extended my index finger, cautiously because sometimes she bites. She hopped on board, encouraged by the popcorn kernel I held just out of her reach.

Since she was in a chatty mood, I tried her out on a

few Socialist slogans, "Workers of the world, unite!" and that ilk, the maxims of my mother's union-organizing life.

"Pretty bird," she said stubbornly, mimicking my Aunt Bea.

"Dumb cluck," I said.

She dug her claws into my finger and got skinny and mean-looking.

"¿Habla Espanol?" I tried, mindful of Paolina's directive.

"Buenas dias," said the bird quite clearly, ruffling up her feathers. God knows what she'd have said if I'd asked her to say buenas dias.

I let her perch on the rim of the popcorn bowl as a tribute to her bilingualism.

My fingers kept wandering to my neck, tracing the faint scratch. It interfered with my appetite, but not until I'd almost emptied the bowl.

I left a few kernels for Esmeralda-Red Emma-Fluffy, dialed Joanne at Area A, and lo!, she picked up the phone.

"Carlotta," she said in an odd voice. I got the feeling she'd been expecting somebody else.

"Busy?" I asked.

"No more than usual," she said too heartily, "But, uh, I haven't got anything on that license plate."

"Nothing? As in zip?"

"I ran it and there's no listing. You probably got the digits mixed up."

"Joanne, that's the plate."

"What can I say, kid? I can't help you on it."

"Can't?"

"That's what I said. Sorry."

I hung up slowly, puzzled because Joanne didn't sound like herself. Puzzled because I knew I'd gotten the damn numbers right. It was a Mass. plate, and the Registry should have had a title to match.

I found the phone book and wrote down Geoffrey Reardon's Somerville address. Then I folded the contract brother Stuart had signed, and stuck it in my handbag. It never hurts to carry an official-looking form.

CHAPTER
22

I had no trouble finding the address, choosing back roads all the way, avoiding lights and traffic like any smart cabbie. It felt good to drive, good to breathe the stale car-heated air. My hands, busy with the wheel, the horn, and the signals, wandered to my neck less frequently.

I stopped across the street from number 85. If Geoff Reardon had committed suicide in the second-floor apartment of this Somerville triple-decker nobody would have wondered why. It looked like the kind of place you rented when you came to the end of the line.

It was a weather-beaten beige house with a bad case

of peeling shingles. Somebody had tried to jazz it up with blue window trim a few decades back, but the window frames were mostly rotted now, sun-faded. Two first-floor windows were cracked and sealed with cardboard to keep out the cold. No great loss; they didn't overlook much of a view. The front lawn was a square brown patch. Narrow burnt-grass alleys separated the house from its closest neighbors. No driveways. A battered big-wheel tricycle rested against a dried-up yew hedge, waiting for some kid to come and play.

I did my reconnoitering from the Toyota. The nearby houses had an abandoned air but were probably crammed with nosy neighbors. In crowded city neighborhoods, you can get away with anything if you look like you know what you're doing. If you look uneasy, uncertain, people get antsy. Sometimes they even call the cops.

Breaking and entering, for that reason alone, should be done under cover of darkness. But I was not about to do a B&E, since I had a perfectly legit key. All I had to do was enter, which can be done in daylight under the right conditions.

I checked out the conditions. The house had two doors: one, more elaborate, for the first floor; the other, a common entry for the second- and third-floor apartments. I could see three separate buzzers, each with a nameplate. I took a deep breath and left the Toyota, my bag slung over my shoulder, the key palmed in my hand.

I don't look much like a burglar. Sometimes it comes in handy.

I went up the porch steps with a purposeful stride,

pretended to hit the third-floor buzzer, waited for a mythical friend to come bouncing downstairs, then, talking to myself, saying things like, "Hi. Gee, it's nice to see you again," I let myself in.

The key turned smoothly in the lock, which helped the illusion. Once inside the narrow foyer, I dropped the smile and the act and tiptoed up the stairs.

I needn't have bothered with the charade. Reardon's neighbors weren't the noticing kind, or else they'd have noticed the person or persons who'd gotten there first and trashed the place.

Not that there was much to trash.

Reardon's office at the Emerson spoke of quiet wealth, old money. His living room talked poverty. His furniture, even before the attentions lavished on it by the intruders, was Morgan Memorial's best. And not much of that. He owned a bilious pink sofa that couldn't have looked a lot better with the pillows whole, and a beige armchair, now lying on its back with one leg stuck in the pseudo fireplace. That was it.

Unless, of course, whoever'd upended the chair had stolen the priceless antiques.

I wondered if the folks on the first and third floors were deaf. They must have heard somebody overturn the chair. Maybe Reardon habitually threw wild parties, but it sure didn't look like that sort of place.

He had a living room, a kitchen, a bath, and a bedroom big enough for a double bed as long as you didn't want to walk around it. The kitchen was a tiny galley with all the appliances lined up against one wall—if you call a two-burner hot plate and a three-by-five mini-refrigerator appliances. There was no oven. Three cupboard doors hung open. The refrigerator contained two cartons of moldy cottage cheese and a half-gallon of milk that I had no desire to sniff.

Somebody'd ripped the sheets and blankets off the bed, and tilted the mattress away from the spring. The lone picture in the entire apartment, a blameless print of Monet's *Water Lilies*, was tossed face down on the bed.

The closet door was closed.

All the other doors in the place were ajar. Every drawer and cupboard, too. I stared at the closet and wished I'd brought my gun instead of rewrapping it in the old undershirt and sticking it in my desk.

Well, I could have gone home, fetched it, come back, and broken in all over again. Instead I crept closer, trying not to creak the wooden floorboards, hugged the wall, turned the doorknob, and flung the sucker open.

Of course, there was nobody inside. It made me feel foolish, taking precautions for nothing. The place was too damn quiet. I wanted to hum or sing or whistle or something, but I kept remembering those first and third-floor tenants.

The closet was dark, bigger than I'd expected, a walk-in. I flicked on the light switch by the side of the door and stepped inside. It was amazing.

At least the size of the bedroom, maybe bigger, it must have started life as a back porch. Somebody'd enclosed it and turned it into the closet of your dreams. Geoff Reardon may not have had furniture, but he had clothes.

I don't know if gay or bisexual men are vainer than the hetero kind. I never conducted a survey. My feeling about alternate lifestyles is generally "live and let live."

Period. Well, maybe there's a twinge of regret because so many good-looking guys are out of the boy-girl market, and so many of my female friends are searching for Mr. Okay, never mind Mr. Right.

I try to take people as I find them, not as representative gays, straights, or whatever. Based on his living quarters alone, Reardon certainly defied stereotype. He was too weird to be typical.

I mean, this was a guy with no oven in his kitchen and eighteen suits in his closet. I counted. Eighteen suits, twenty sports coats—all hung on fancy wooden hangers. He had a valet press and a revolving tie rack. Enough shoes to stock a small shop, complete with wooden shoe trees. Wire baskets, two full of sweaters, one of brightly colored skimpy jockey shorts, lined the walls. Shirts were piled high in cardboard laundry boxes.

Somebody had poked around, emptied a few shirt boxes, pushed aside a few hangers, but there was no destruction. Not like in the living room.

I backed out and sat on the edge of the bed.

Okay. Somebody had beat me to it. But who?

Robbers read the obits. That's a fact of life. If your hubby dies and you give the press the time and date of the funeral, you are advertising your absence from home, and there are some jerks out there who'll take the opportunity to add to your grief. I used to see it all the time when I was a cop.

So it could have been your ordinary grave robbers.

It could have been a lover, removing a bawdy photograph, a compromising letter. Would an ex-lover slit the sofa cushions?

Reardon could have been mixed up in some drug and

sex thing at the school, like Valerie's father suspected, and one of his partners could have searched for his stash of dope or kiddie porn. The old falling-out-among-thieves routine.

Whoever trashed the place probably hadn't been looking for Valerie's notebook.

Which meant I might as well look for it myself.

I went through that place like cops are supposed to after a suspicious death. I practically counted the knives and forks. I found little of a personal nature. No photos. No knickknacks. Certainly no compromising photos or letters. I wondered if Reardon had gotten rid of things prior to his suicide. I sure would. It's bad enough to die, but think of some cop going through your stuff afterward.

Did I find the notebook?

No.

A still small voice at the back of my head wondered if Reardon had returned it to Valerie. And when.

CHAPTER
24

I picked up a cab at ten Sunday night.

Earlier, I'd phoned Mooney.

He sounded like I woke him up, which worried me because eight o'clock is early for a grown man to hit the sack alone, probably a sign of depression. I suppose I should have been glad he was home instead of drinking in some bar. I asked how things were going, and he grunted a reply.

"Cops found your witness yet?" I asked.

"If they have, they haven't told me. Or the *Herald*. Hearing's coming up fast."

"Stop reading the papers," I said. "Look, Mooney, you know Joanne. Anything funny with her?"

"Triola? Nope. Why?"

"I asked her to run a plate and she's giving me the runaround."

"The P.D. doesn't exist to do you favors. Ever think of that?" he asked, sounding more like himself.

"Nope. How about you?"

"How about me what?"

"How are you on doing me favors?"

"Like?"

"A guy killed himself in Lincoln. I'd like to know details."

"So?"

"You know somebody in Lincoln?"

"I might," Mooney said, always cautious.

"A cop?"

"Yeah."

"Can you see where I'm headed, Mooney?"

"You want me to ask him about this stiff."

"Geoffrey Reardon," I said. "With a G. Got that?"

"How much do I owe you so far?" he asked. "For looking for that damn hooker?"

"Nothing. I haven't found her."

"I sent you a check."

"Geez," I said, "I never got it. You'd better stop payment."

"Carlotta," he said.

"You can work off your debt finding out about Reardon," I said.

"Yeah, well, my cop friend might not be so forthcoming if he knows I'm—"

"How's he gonna know you're suspended?" I said quickly.

"Seems to me everybody knows."

"Yeah," I said. "Well, Gloria sends you her best."

"See, she knows."

"What Gloria doesn't know," I said, "isn't worth knowing."

That much was true. She sat in her wheelchair, a busy spider connected to a web of radios and telephones, absorbing information as fast as she swallowed Twinkies. She was an encyclopedia of city lore and fast becoming legend in the tight world of Boston cabs.

For instance, she knew I was coming over. That's why she saved a bone-rattler especially for me.

I cabbed it into the Zone and hung out till midnight, keeping warm with a Chris Smither tape and two pairs of gloves, seeing lots of familiar faces but no one remotely like Janine, the tattooed lady.

I kept an eye out for my gray Chevy Caprice, too. No luck.

I wondered what Mooney would be able to learn in Lincoln. I thought about Stuart Reardon and traced the scratch on my throat. What if I were responsible, indirectly, for Reardon's suicide? I mean, maybe brother Stuart hadn't been so far off course. Maybe Geoff had started something with Valerie, an affair that, once discovered, would get him fired, or worse.

Since I wasn't looking for her, I almost passed right by. I had to circle the block in rising excitement while I pried the photo out of my purse. It was Valerie Haslam, dressed and made up to kill, prancing along Washington Street on four-inch spikes.

Which was strange because she was supposed to be home in Lincoln.

I was deciding on an approach when the radio grumbled and erupted. It was Gloria's deep contralto. I answered and she said: "Sam's here, and he's got an ID on that plate."

"Look, Glory, I'm onto something and I can't take it now."

"Okay," she said, "Call back soon then, babe."

"Will do," I said.

"Real soon," she said. "And watch your butt."

CHAPTER
25

I took the last corner too fast, screeching the wheels because I was afraid my quarry would get picked up during the two minutes it took me to circle the block. I was more than intrigued by Valerie's presence in the Zone.

I wanted to meet this teenage femme fatale, this fourteen-year-old who evoked such varied responses from the people closest to her. Who the hell would she be, I wondered? The competent young woman capable of taking charge of her life, the one I'd heard about from Elsie McLintock?

Or the innocent who'd run away because the boy next door had pawed her behind the math building?

Or the stubborn child, resistant to all her well-meaning parents could do, running to the Combat Zone in search of something she couldn't find at the elegant Emerson School?

Would Valerie be the girl of Geoffrey Reardon's fantasies, shy and strange, wild and free? A poet without words, a dancer minus technique?

Who was this girl who'd run away again, this little painted tramp, this daughter, this student, this friend?

"You!"

I rolled down the window, pulled up close to the curb, and hollered. Valerie pivoted with a come-hither smile on her lips. It faded. She stared at me, then shook her head no. Her tongue protruded between scarlet lips.

"No chicks," she said curtly. The makeup couldn't disguise her youth.

"Get in the cab," I said.

"You crazy?" she responded. "Deaf? Fuck off."

I should have faked her, should have told her I was playing Stepin Fetchit for some rich, weird john who didn't do his own cruising, but I was only using half my mind. The other half was pondering Gloria's message, hoping Sam had told her something that would help me pull Mooney out of his hole.

"Get in the cab, Valerie," I said. "Jerry's worried about you."

That got her attention. "Jerry?" she repeated.

"Your mom and dad, too."

She moved fast for a girl wearing high heels, a tight miniskirt, and enough junk jewelry to sink a rowboat.

For a block she stuck to the street and I tailed her in the car. Then she veered down a narrow walkway between two buildings, and I had no choice but to tromp the brakes and leave the cab in a loading zone. I took an extra two seconds to lock up, because I figured if I lost another cab, Gloria would be truly pissed.

Not to mention Sam.

Valerie had a city block lead by the time I hit the street. My sneakers cut the distance. I was doing fine, ten feet behind and closing, when she ducked into a building and screwed it all up.

After midnight most places close down, right? But not hospitals, and Valerie had blundered into one of Boston's biggest, the New England Medical Center, a bewildering array of buildings connected by tunnels, bridges, walkways, and God knows what. If a fare asked for New England Medical Center, you could drop him or her at any one of a dozen entrances, and still be well within the Center. They probably had to run a shuttle bus.

"Come back," I shouted, which was a waste of breath. She couldn't have heard me, and if she had, she wouldn't have listened.

The uniformed guard sitting at a tiny oak desk must have been half-asleep when Valerie went tearing by. He stared at me open-mouthed and started to rise.

I hate hospitals. I don't enter them by choice. The antiseptic smell makes my spine crawl. The rooms look like cells and the nurses like prison guards.

But damned if I was going to let that girl get away.

"Emergency," I yelled, cradling my arm as if it were broken. Then I ran, leaving the gape-mouthed guard behind me.

We scooted down fluorescent-lit hallways, some gray and placid, some crowded with medieval torture apparatus. Doors were flung wide in our wake and occasionally somebody shouted. I focused on Valerie and nothing else. Her purse, a tiny contraption no bigger than a wallet and attached to a long strap that bandoliered her shoulder, banged rhythmically against her hip.

It was her five-four in heels against my six-one in sneakers. If it hadn't been for all the corners she wouldn't have had a prayer. When she turned I could hear her pounding steps on the polished floor. We were starting to cause quite a stir among fresh-faced interns and weary nurses. We passed another desk and I could see phones fly to faces, hear the cry for Security.

She cut a ninety-degree angle and raced down a hallway lined with IV stands and wheelchairs toward a door with a red Exit sign overhead. By the time I got there the door was closed and her heels were tapping upstairs. I took the stairs two at a time, but the door on the next landing slammed shut just as I got there. She was out on the second floor.

We played tag through the corridors. The second floor seemed to be arranged like a four-leaf clover, but the outer edge of each petal had a walkway to the outer edge of the next so I couldn't trap her in a dead end. I kept my eyes glued to her fleeing back and fumbled with the zipper on my down vest. The air was hot and still, stifling after the frigid outdoors, and I was starting to drip sweat.

Suddenly I couldn't see her anymore, couldn't hear her. I did a quick three-sixty and caught sight of her maybe twenty feet away, just stepping into an elevator.

Shit. I reversed direction so fast my heels skidded. Once the elevator doors closed she was gone. She could get out on any floor. I'd lose her. I felt like I was running through maple syrup, getting nowhere as the doors started to close. They seemed to work in slow motion, gradually narrowing the gap. I could see Valerie pressed against the back of the car, her scarlet lips open. I threw myself across the floor like I was diving for a distant volleyball on the crucial point of a championship match. The doors closed on my right wrist, balked, and opened.

I picked myself up and walked in.

Valerie wasn't alone in the elevator. There was the tiniest shriveled-up old man tucked in the corner grasping a cane. He wore glasses with lenses so thick they made his eyes look froglike. He turned slowly from me to Valerie, Valerie to me. His hands shook.

In a shivery ancient voice he said, "Up or down?"

"Down," I said.

The elevator silence was punctuated with breathing. Valerie was gulping air as hard as I was. The old man's breath rasped through his nose.

I took Valerie's arm, smiled grimly, and said, "When the doors open, we're going to walk quietly out the nearest exit."

"I'll scream," she whispered furiously.

"Scream and I promise you'll spend the night in a cell," I said conversationally, squeezing her arm a little tighter. The old man inched toward the doors, leaning heavily on the cane. I dragged Valerie a step forward and punched the hold button so the doors wouldn't shut on him. He kept his eyes glued on the floor, his lips pursed in concentration. "Ever seen the cells they dump the hookers in?" I asked. "Ever smelled 'em?"

"I won't go home," she said.

I took her purse by the shoulder strap, transferred it to my handbag, which was big enough to swallow it whole and a few more besides.

"Hey—" she protested.

"It's just to ensure you come along," I said. "You'll get it back."

"I won't go home," she repeated.

"We'll talk about it," I said. The old man cleared the doorway, his halting shuffle propelling him at a crawl.

The security guard wasn't at his desk. He must have been called away.

CHAPTER
26

It seemed like miles back to the cab. Valerie didn't exactly fight me, but she wasn't all that helpful either. For somebody who could move so fast, she walked slowly. Once she tried to wriggle away and I had to grab her by the hair.

The cab was where I'd left it. In Boston, the stolen-car capital of the western world, that is not always the case.

Cops carry handcuffs. Private investigators don't. Nor do they have the option of tossing prisoners into a caged back seat bereft of door handles.

I kept Valerie with me in the front seat, in the middle straddling the hump, not on the passenger side. That way she'd need to scoot over, avoid banging into the fare meter, unlock the door, and heave it open before escaping. And by that time I'd stop her.

She didn't try anything. She was still breathing hard from the chase, and after that last wriggle she seemed to lose heart. Maybe she didn't like having her hair pulled.

I watched her more closely than I watched the road. There wasn't much traffic.

She'd stuck some kind of gunk on the front of her hair to make it stand on end, and she'd overdone her makeup in bold colored triangles. The effect was punk, bizarre, and cheap. She wore a low-cut Spandex bodysuit in metallic silver paired with a thigh-high black mini and killer heels. Red plastic beads, matching dangle earrings, and a fistful of rings completed the ensemble. I wondered if she'd worn the bodysuit in Geoff Reardon's class.

It wasn't her attire that separated her from the young girl in the school photo. It was her eyes. This version of Valerie had defiant, alert eyes, alive and glowing, eyes that wouldn't look demurely away from the camera.

"You on drugs?" I asked. I learned the technique when I was a cop. Often the blunt unexpected inquiry will net more response than measured logic.

"Nah," she said. "I do some coke, but so does everybody. I don't need it."

"Yeah," I said. "Well, you run pretty fast."

"Not as fast as you."

"Next time you're going to race me, dump the shoes," I said.

She looked down at her feet and stifled a giggle. "I never thought of that."

"You're lucky you didn't break a leg," I said.

"Lucky," she repeated sarcastically. "Well, at least I'd have been in a hospital. Look, can't we just forget you saw me?"

"Sorry," I said.

"You a cop?"

"Private," I said.

"I could pay you," she said.

"With what you turn in tricks?" I asked.

She ignored that for a while, but I could hear her ragged breathing. Then she said, "You mind if I turn on some noise?" Her voice was a blast of arctic air.

"Go ahead," I said. "There's a tape in the player."

The music picked up in the middle of Rory Block's "Lovin' Whiskey," so I reached over and punched rewind.

It's a sad wailing song about loving a guy who drinks, and Block sings it with feeling and grace and a fine guitar backup. I don't know much about coping with alcoholics, but I know a lot about living with a coke-fiend, and believe me, she's got it right.

I stole a glance at Valerie. A tear had worked its way down her cheek, leaving a glistening trail edged in black mascara.

"Hey," I said.

She turned her face to the window.

"Sorry," I said.

"Look, I mean it when I say I won't go home."

"I believe you," I said.

"So where are we going?" she asked.

"It's late," I said. "We'll go to my place."

"Where's that?"

"Cambridge."

"Will you call my father?"

"We'll talk about it," I said.

We stopped by Green & White to swap for my Toyota, and she didn't try anything there. Sam's car wasn't parked in the lot, and Gloria was swamped with the phones, so I didn't pick up the message about the license plate. I figured I'd call once I got home.

But sitting on my front porch was a man I'd never expected to see there again.

Sam Gianelli.

CHAPTER
27

S hit," said Valerie Haslam, her face pressed against the passenger window. "Is that your boyfriend or something?"

"Something," I said, feeling unaccustomed warmth spread across my face.

"Shit," she repeated under her breath, and we exchanged brief speculative smiles. She had great teeth, expensive orthodontist-improved rich-girl teeth. For the barest second, behind the garish green eye shadow, she looked like a regular teenager.

"When I stop the car," I said, "come out my side."

"I'm not going to run," she said.

I guess she wanted to see Sam close up. I didn't blame her. "Glad to hear it," I said.

"Well, you've got my fuckin' purse," she said.

"Yeah," I said. "I'm fuckin' impressed. Let's go."

I kept my hand on her arm, jailer-style, all the way up the front walk. I never seem to see Sam under remotely normal conditions.

"Hi," he said.

"Hi," I said.

"Hang on," I rang the front bell three times and hoped like hell Roz was home, reasonably dressed, and not busy screwing the plumber. I was delighted to hear her feet clatter down the stairs.

"Forget your key?" she said when she opened the door. Then she looked around me and was struck dumb by the sight of Sam. She always approved of Sam. Said he had a great body. Which he has.

"Roz, meet Valerie. Take her in the kitchen and feed her, okay? And keep her there. She runs."

"I'm not hungry," Valerie protested. She wanted to stay with the adults, I could tell.

"Better still," I said. "Take her upstairs to my room and keep her there."

"Yeah," Roz said. "March."

"She's tricky," I warned.

Valerie smiled at that. She also smiled at Sam, testing out her feminine allure and three layers of mascara.

"So am I," Roz said. "So long."

That left me and Sam freezing on the porch. I was very aware of my disheveled hair and the dried sweat on my back.

"Can I come in?" he said.

"Sure," I said, making it into the foyer without stumbling over the front step. So did he.

"I've got news," he said, while I said, "Gloria told me—"

We both came to abrupt halts.

"Go ahead," I said.

"No, you," he said.

"Thanks for getting the license plate."

"Did Gloria tell you—"

"Just that you got the plate."

"She should have—" he started, while I chimed in with, "I was too busy to—"

We both stopped again.

"Listen, Carlotta," he said, "the plate you gave me belongs to an undercover cop car."

It took a while to sink in. "Are you sure?" I said.

He nodded.

"Shit," I said. I wandered into the living room and sank into Aunt Bea's rocker. I never sit there.

"There's more, not much."

"Would you like to sit down?" I said, standing again, suddenly aware that I'd been staring at him. "Have a beer or something."

"Yeah," he said, walking around the living room. "The place looks good."

"It's okay."

"You look good," he said.

He followed me into the kitchen. Close. I don't know how he was feeling but I was having trouble keeping my hands to myself. Sam has that effect on me. I think I have that effect on him. I used to. It's like a danger signal, red, pulsing, and overwhelming. I hadn't been alone in a room with him for seven months.

"Carlotta." He put his hands on my shoulders and I froze. Then he turned me around, and walked me backward until my back pressed up against the refrigerator. I cooperated.

"Jesus, your hair smells good," he said.

"Sam," was all I could manage because the smell of him, the combination of shampoo and after-shave and Sam was just the same, and it hit me hard, in the stomach and below.

"It's been a long time," he said.

"Yeah," I said. His hands were busy on my shoulders and my neck.

"I missed you," he said.

"Yeah," I muttered. It was the only sound I could make.

"Look, Carlotta, what happened, happened. It really didn't have anything to do with you and me. We were just there, right?"

"We sure were."

"I thought you were using me, to get close to G&W."

"I thought you were using me."

"Are we even?" he asked, rubbing his fingers on my cheek.

"Even," I said.

"So what do we do now," he said. "Now that we're even."

"Want a drink?" I said.

He leaned down and kissed me, one of those soft, melting kisses that calls for an immediate, more urgent encore, and another.

After a while I surfaced and said, "This is not what you call great timing. I've got a runaway upstairs and a cop car involved in God knows what and I don't have time to—"

He kissed me again and I went along for the ride.

"Sam," I said. "I hate to do this, but I need to know what you found out, and I need to talk to this kid upstairs, and what I'm telling you, Sam, is I need a rain check." This took me a while to spit out because we were busy kissing and pawing each other. He smelled wonderful, tasted wonderful. I was breathing faster than I had during the chase.

"Sam," I said, putting some muscle behind it. "Sam, back off. Sit down. Tell me what's going on."

"I don't think I can move," he said. "I'm pinned."

"Sit," I said with a grin. "I'll pour a beer on it."

"You haven't changed," he said. "Except probably you're in worse trouble."

"Tell me about it," I said.

So we sat at the kitchen table and drank beer and tried to keep our hands off each other.

"My friend got the name of the cop who usually uses the unit. It's one of the old turds from Area D. Joe Manelli. You know him?"

"Manelli, Manelli, Manelli," I mumbled. "Sounds familiar."

"He's not one of your more honest cops."

Anybody else says that about a cop, I get pissed. Sam says it, he knows. His sources of information are incredibly reliable. People don't lie to Sam Gianelli. He might tell Papa. Of course, he wouldn't—he doesn't even speak to Papa—but the stooges don't know that.

"Shit," I said, banging my fist on the table. "Manelli!"

"It means something."

"Christ, Sam, it means everything. Thank you. I mean it. Thank you." Manelli was the guy at the Blue Note, the one who'd poured scotch on the floor. In a sudden flash, I saw him leaving the bar, and recognized him as the man with the greasy hair and narrow shoulders, the driver of the gray Caprice.

If the Caprice was an undercover unit, it would have a police radio, standard issue. Manelli could have noticed me tailing him, called for somebody to take me out . . .

"You gotta go now, Sam," I said. "I've got work."

"It's bedtime," he said.

"I wish," I said. "Honest, Sam. I wish. Do me a favor and go home before I jump you."

"Hell," he said. "Why should I?"

"Please," I said.

So we kissed some more, like frustrated teenagers in Mom's back room, and he left.

Sex. It can overwhelm your better judgment.

CHAPTER
28

After Sam left, I breathed for a while. Then I hollered up to Roz to make sure things were under control. They were, so I dialed a number I know by heart, and gave the extension for the detective's squad room. An unfamiliar voice picked up after eight rings. I asked for Detective Triola.

"Hang on," the voice said. "I think she's around here somewhere."

I blew out a sigh of relief and three minutes later Joanne came on the line. "Triola," she said crisply.

"Jo," I said, "It's Carlotta."

"Carlotta, I told you—"

"Look, I know about the car. It's an undercover unit, and you think you can't talk to me about it because it's police business and all that crap, but once you hear the whole story, you'll be glad to talk—if you want to get Mooney off the hook."

"You know I do," she said cautiously.

"The plate belongs to a car I tailed through Franklin Park. Mooney's missing witness was inside, also two guys I thought were johns, okay? I'd been on them for maybe fifteen minutes when I caught a tail of my own. Now if the car was an undercover, they could have radioed for backup—the kind of backup that ran me off the road."

"Shit," Joanne said.

"It might help Mooney if you check the police garage, see if anybody brought a unit in for front-end repairs."

"They wouldn't be that dumb," Jo said.

"What would you suggest?"

"There's a lot of background noise here," Jo said softly, "but I think I ought to talk to IA."

"You know somebody clean?"

"I think so," she said after a long pause. When you're dealing with crooked cops you have to be damn careful. Cops have friends. They're all connected in some kind of network. Jo wouldn't want to take her case to Manelli's brother-in-law.

"If you could get a tail on Manelli, I think he'd lead you to Mooney's witness."

"Got a name on the witness?"

"Just a first. Janine. Hooker. Lots of paper on her. Does decal tattoos. Blonde. Caucasian. Five-five. Renney used to pimp for her."

"I'll see what I can do," Joanne said.

"Jo, can you get Mooney in on this?"

"Shit, Carlotta, it's kind of delicate, you know."

"But you'll try."

"You don't ask much."

"I know. Look, I'm gonna call him now. I'll let him know you'll be in touch, okay?"

"You're jumping the gun, Carlotta."

"I gotta go now, Jo. Thanks for everything." I slammed the receiver down quickly because I knew she'd want to dicker, and I didn't have the time. I needed to talk to Mooney and I needed to get upstairs to Valerie. I dialed, hoping I wouldn't wake Mooney's mother.

"Hello?" His voice was thick with sleep.

"Mooney," I said. "Carlotta. I've got to know some stuff quick."

"Carlotta?" he said. "It's—"

"It's late, I know, but this is important."

"It better be."

"Get your feet on the floor, Moon, and pay attention."

"Are you okay?" he said. "Your voice sounds kind of funny, like you been running."

"I have," I said. It wasn't really a lie and I didn't want to tell him I was still practically panting from my encounter with Sam.

"Okay," he said. "I'm up. Shoot."

"Joe Manelli," I said. "Area D. Is he one of the cops you testified against on the bar scam?"

"Carlotta—"

"Don't even try to tell me it's departmental business, Moon. It's your business, believe me."

"What if he is?" Mooney said, always cautious.

Bingo.

"Would it interest you," I said, "to know that I saw him twice this week, once at the Blue Note and once with a tattooed woman?"

"Huh?"

"Mooney, how did your testimony go over? At the bar scam hearing."

"What do you expect?" he said bitterly. "One crooked cop accusing another crooked cop, that's the way they looked at me."

"That's what Manelli did to you," I said. "He's hiding your witness. He's got her stashed somewhere till after the hearings. He's real friendly with the people at the Blue Note, probably been arranging protection for them all along. Somebody must have called him as soon as the fight went down. He bought the witnesses, and snitched the one who wouldn't shut up. So you'd look bad, Mooney."

"Jesus," Mooney said.

"Yeah," I said.

"A cop," he said.

"Where would Manelli stash a witness, Mooney? That's what you've got to find out."

"I'll kill the bastard," Mooney said.

"Not a good idea."

"What he put me through, what he put my mother through—"

"Let him rot in jail, Mooney," I said. "It's better."

"Maybe," he said, but he didn't sound convinced.

"Mooney, we're gonna find her. I've already talked to Triola, and she's going to Internal Affairs. If Manelli can stash her, you and me and Jo can find her, right? Am I right?"

"Yeah," he said.

"Triola's going to handle it. She'll call you. Be sure to tell her the whole thing, about Manelli and the bars and your testimony. She's going to get the honest cops on your side."

He didn't say a word. I could hear him breathing.

"Mooney," I said, "Much as I hate to change the subject, did you find out anything about my Lincoln suicide?"

"Shit, Carlotta, I'd have called. Maybe not at three in the morning. But I'd have called."

"What did they say?"

"Straightforward suicide."

"Aw, Mooney, don't tell me that Tell me something suspicious, something weird."

"That's why you got bounced from the force, you know, Carlotta. Gotta make everything weird."

"I have a suspicious nature, Mooney. You know that."

"I guess," he said with the first hint of a smile in his voice.

"So what gives?"

"I got a copy of the coroner's report."

"Good. Now what's in it that invites speculation?"

"No funny stuff. I mean it. Death by carbon monoxide inhalation. You probably don't need to know the number of parts per thousand. There was a bruise on the side of the guy's head but the medical examiner figures that's where he banged his head when he fell against the side door. No note, either, but the file's practically nailed shut. That school has clout and they don't want it open."

"Thanks," I said.

"For what?" he said.

"You'll see."

"Manelli," he said.

"He saw a way out of his own jam, Mooney, and he took it."

"He's supposed to be a *cop*," Mooney said.

"Yeah," I agreed.

"I'm not gonna be able to sleep," he said. "Leaves a bad taste in my mouth, you know."

"Yeah. I'm sorry."

"Hell, you got nothing to be sorry for. Here I been relying on the cops to save my ass. I'm not gonna sleep," he repeated.

"Yeah," I said.

"I don't suppose you'd like some company?" he asked.

"Oh, Mooney," I said. "Not tonight."

CHAPTER
29

"This babe is one hard case," Roz declared when I came up the stairs. The way she said it, she didn't mean it. Roz is tough enough to know.

Valerie had made herself at home in my room to the extent of sprawling across the unmade bed. I never make my bed. She'd taken off her heels and tossed them across the room. Her face was buried in my pillows.

"Drugs?" I asked Roz.

"No tracks," Roz said. "I think she's just tired and cold. Maybe she's hungry but she won't eat. She's major-league pissed. Took a swing at me."

I didn't have to ask if it had connected. Roz is fast.

"Okay," I said. "Thanks. I'll take over now."

"Sam still here?" she asked.

"Nope," I said.

"Too bad."

"Yeah." My response was heartfelt.

"If you need me," Roz said.

"Yeah," I said again.

"Take care," Roz said to the girl on the bed. Valerie snorted. Roz left.

"My name's Carlotta," I said.

Nothing.

"Roz is gone. I'm here. The dame who runs faster than you."

"Not if I have my shoes off," she said. At least I think that's what she said. It was pillow-muffled.

"When did you take off again?"

She turned her face. Her mascara was all smeary. Cross off one pillow case.

"I don't know what you mean," she said.

"Let's try this one," I said. "Where's your diary?"

"Huh?" she said blankly. "What do you care? My diary?"

"The thing you kept for Reardon's class."

"Oh."

"Where is it?" I asked.

"How the hell should I know?"

"You turned it in to Reardon."

"So what?" she said, elaborately unconcerned.

"Was there stuff in there about running away?"

"Yeah, I guess."

"Is that why you went back to get it?" I asked.

"Huh?"

"Am I going to have to repeat everything I say?"

"Go back to the goddamn Emerson? I wouldn't go back there."

"Not even the day Reardon died?"

She stared at me. Her mouth did something funny, then it turned up at the corners.

"Come on," she said.

"What?"

"That's not funny," she said. "Christ."

"Didn't your father tell you?"

"My *father*? You don't make any sense at all."

"Likewise," I said.

"Are you going to tell my parents where I am?"

"I'll probably call," I said cautiously. "Parents have a way of worrying. Did you just walk out this time, or did you leave a note?"

"Leave a note?" she said incredulously. "Why didn't you ask them that? You're working for them."

"I haven't talked to them since Reardon died."

"Stop saying that."

"What?"

"Look, I've been gone more than two weeks, for Christ's sake. I was doing okay."

"Back up," I said. "You didn't go home?"

"I'm never going home. Except to get my sister. Once I get set up, once I get a place, I'm going to get Sherri."

"You saw Geoff Reardon in the Combat Zone," I said, backtracking. I wanted to see if she was lying for the hell of it.

"Yeah," she said. "He read my stupid notebook and he wanted to talk. He's okay, you know, for a teacher. He's special. I mean, aside from being so gorgeous. He was gonna help me. He gave me some money. He said he was gonna come back and give me more, a lot more. A couple thousand, he said, but I don't know where he was gonna get it. I mean, teachers don't make much, do they? It would have been enough for bus tickets out west, and a security deposit on an apartment. You need two months' rent for a security deposit. It's a lot of dough."

"Your father didn't see you this week?" I said.

"That jerk. No."

"And you didn't see Reardon?"

"No."

"And you don't know he's dead."

"Why do you keep saying that?" she asked anxiously.

"It's true," I said. "That's why."

"Please," she said.

"I'm sorry," I said.

"Dead," she repeated.

"Yeah."

"How?"

"He killed himself."

"Oh, no," she said. "That's dumb. He wouldn't."

"The police say he did."

"But—"

I shook my head and her face crumbled. She flung herself down on the pillow. Her shoulders shook, but she didn't make any noise. I went over and patted her on the back. At first she recoiled from my touch, then she lay still. I would have stayed with her except I heard Roz yell for help.

CHAPTER
30

Roz is not a screamer. I don't mean she's quiet. Particularly when using one of her tumbling mats for love-making, she can turn out the most incredible progression of provoking noises. But this was something different, and I was out of the bedroom before I thought about what the trouble might be.

She had tried the second-floor bathroom. I don't know if her lover, the tall, dumb plumber had told her it was safe in some fit of overconfidence, or her nonlover, in a corresponding fit of jealous rage, had told her the same, but Roz was stuck in the bathroom, staring transfixed at the geyser erupting from the ruptured faucet of the Day-Glo orange sink.

She was soaked, dripping, huddled on the window side of the bathroom. To get to the door she would have had to run under the fountain. Steam was rising.

"Shut-off valve!" I yelled.

"It's under the fucking sink," she screamed. "Too hot."

"Don't move," I said.

"I'm going out the window," she cried.

"Is it hitting you?"

"No, but the steam—"

"This is the second floor," I shouted. "Stay there."

"I can jump," she said.

"There aren't any fucking tumbling mats. I'll get the shut-off in the basement."

"Hurry," she said.

I was already down the stairs. Every time I took a step I muttered something about the Twin Brothers. Stupid, shitty, dumb-ass, motherfucking Twin Brothers.

I had to find a flashlight, race down two flights of stairs, remember where the damn shut-off valve was, all the while hoping Roz didn't scald herself to death or crawl out the window and crash to the ground.

When I ran back up, the first words Roz screamed, peering over the landing, were, "Did you catch her?"

Valerie. She was goddamn gone.

CHAPTER
31

The bathroom was a disaster, a swamp of steamy water and warping chocolate tiles, like squares of Hershey left out in the sun. Water dripped from ceiling tiles that would never be the same color again. The battered faucet of the Day-Glo orange sink clogged its porcelain bowl.

Roz, now standing in the hallway hanging her head, had wisely closed the door when she ran out. I was sorry I'd reopened it.

"Shit," I said, plunging my hand in the sink and yanking out the chunk of faucet. The water drained with a vengeful sucking noise. I went to dry off my hand but the towels were all soaked.

My hand may have been dripping hot water, but the rest of me was freezing. At Roz's shouted warning, I'd run out of the house without my coat, searching for Valerie. In the dark my neighborhood of close-together houses and hearty oaks could have hidden an army. "Valerie," I shouted, imagining her silent, scornful laughter as she hid behind a bush or in the shadow of a nearby porch or tool shed.

"Goddammit," I said, wiping my hand on my jeans.

Abandoning the bathroom, I ran to get my outdoor clothes, my shoulder bag, a strong flashlight. The girl couldn't have gotten far. With my car . . .

That's when I heard the motor start, and the character and direction of the noise made my heart stop. I stared at the front door and realized what I hadn't noticed before. Valerie had left the door swung wide on its hinges. I'd closed it on my first fruitless return. My keys, left in the lock, were gone. I ran to the front door fast enough to see my car, my dear red Toyota, my first and only car, drive away without me.

"Shit," I said.

So I was wet, freezing, angry, and feeling pretty dumb to boot. I thought about calling the cops to report my stolen car but couldn't bear the monumental indifference with which the Cambridge Police would greet the news.

Car theft is a misdemeanor in this state unless the owner can prove that whoever stole the vehicle did so with intent to deprive said owner of use on a permanent basis. A kid taking a joyride isn't really a car thief under Massachusetts law.

I sent upward a brief but fervent prayer that Valerie, underage though she was, had some rudimentary knowledge of the driving process.

I grabbed my handbag to get the car registration. It felt unusually heavy, and I remembered Valerie's purse, her wallet-sized shoulder bag, stuffed deep into its nether regions.

I found it and tumbled its contents onto the kitchen table. Two lipsticks rolled to the floor. Subway tokens joined them. There was a package of condoms in among the wadded Kleenex, and a pack of cigarettes. Virginia Slims. Two matchbook folders, both from Zone bars. No address book. There were various keys, but none with an ID tag. I'd been hoping for a hotel key. A rich little bitch like her would have rented a room.

Folded up small was a piece of paper, lined notebook paper torn at the margin, a page filled with round childish writing. I read it. I sat down. I read it again.

The page had been ripped in two. The top half was lost so there was no lead-in to the meat of the paragraph.

. . . so I dream about running away. To places where they know what I am, where the girls are like me. Or I dream about telling Jerry. Or telling you. Telling everybody. Just walking to the front of the stage someday and saying in my quiet voice that I haven't ever been a virgin. I don't remember being a virgin because my father is my lover and he has always been since I can remember. And if I say no he says he will do it to Sherri and that I'm the oldest and I can take it best. And if I say I'll tell my mother he says it will kill her and if I tell anyone else he will kill them and if anyone finds out no boy will ever want to marry me and I care about that even though I don't know why because I don't want to marry anybody like my father ever ever ever ever ever ever ever ever ever ever ever ever ever ever ever ever ever ever ever ever ever . . .

She'd written that one word over and over, maybe a hundred times. It took up a third of the page and ran over and filled up the back getting heavier and blacker. A cry even a self-centered man like Geoff Reardon couldn't ignore.

He hadn't ignored it. He'd sought out Valerie. He'd promised her money. Money from where? And he was going to stop teaching, maybe have the money to produce his play. . . .

I rubbed my hand across my dry lips and caught myself wondering if I'd shaken Prescott Haslam's hand, if I'd touched his hand with mine.

Valerie hadn't known about Reardon's death until I told her.

I reread the notebook page, found the fragment I remembered:

. . . if I tell anyone else he will kill them . . .

Valerie hadn't returned home the day of Reardon's death. Reardon had promised to help the girl financially.

And now Valerie had taken my car. Why? Here in Cambridge, she could catch any Red Line train back to the Zone.

"Roz," I yelled.

Then I ran into the living room, unlocked my bottom desk drawer, and hurriedly unwrapped my gun. The sharp, oily smell hit me like icy water, and I hoped I was wrong about where Valerie was headed. I hollered for Roz again as I finished loading and tucked the .38 in the pocket of my coat.

I hadn't heard her come down the stairs. She was barefoot in a white terry robe, with a big maroon towel wound around her head.

"They're coming over," she said defensively, before I had a chance to speak. "They're on their way. It won't be five minutes."

"Who?" I said.

"The Brothers. They don't understand how it could have happened. They'll fix everything."

"Sure they will," I said.

I was pacing by the time the truck finally squealed to a halt in front of the house.

Roz convinced them to let me borrow it. After the fact. I just snatched their keys and took off.

CHAPTER
32

One-fifteen Lilac Palace Road, Lincoln.

I had a hell of a time finding it. No streetlamps, and if there'd been any they wouldn't have helped much because few of the corners boasted street signs.

I had to keep pulling off to the side of the road, checking the Arrow Streetguide for the Towns of Eastern Mass. that the Twin Brothers kept in their dash compartment.

That it came equipped with a street guide was the only good word about the Twin Brothers' truck. It didn't have a dome light, so I had to keep yanking out my flash to read the maps. Its less-than-luxurious interior and rotten smell aside, it couldn't corner worth a damn, and its steering made Gloria's orneriest cab seem like a Porsche 944. I nursed it up to forty-eight m.p.h. on Route 2, and thought the shaking would knock out my fillings. It was a good thing it couldn't go any faster because the brakes were minimal, which I discovered after inadvertently running a red. The Brothers could probably claim antique status for both the shocks and the muffler.

As I drove Valerie's words kept echoing. *I've never been a virgin. My father is my lover.* In their initial impact, I'd accepted them without question. Now I found myself doubting. Was Valerie telling the truth? She'd written the words for her drama teacher. Was her incest claim an attention-seeking ploy, a theatrical lie?

I pictured the man I'd met over Chinese food, the bespectacled stockbroker, Preston Haslam. I heard his cool voice on my answering machine, declaring his daughter safely home. I saw Valerie, eye makeup streaked, crying on my unmade bed. I believed the girl. Why? Because she'd run away after handing in her diary, unable to bear the thought that her teacher would know her shame. Because she'd fallen apart when Jerry Toland kissed her.

And most of all, because it explained Geoff Reardon's death, made it murder instead of unmotivated suicide. After reading Valerie's diary, Reardon had sought her out in the Zone. Promised her help. Money. Thousands of dollars, Valerie had claimed, even while she wondered where the teacher would get that kind of cash. Where else? He must have gone to Haslam, promised to tell his dirty secret unless the stockbroker came up with money—enough to help Valerie, enough to let Reardon retire from teaching. Haslam must have been the angel who was planning to invest in Reardon's screenplay. . . .

Maybe Reardon had overestimated Haslam's wealth, asked for an impossible amount. Maybe he'd just underestimated Haslam's need to keep his secret.

I didn't find 115 Lilac Palace Road so much as I found my car, my dear Toyota, pulled to the side of a road I thought might be Lilac Palace. It rested at an angle with the front tires on the grass verge and the back tires well into the street. Not well parked, but I couldn't see any dents. Valerie hadn't locked the front door, but the key was gone from the ignition.

I'd had to wait for the plumbers' truck and it had taken me some time to find the place. Valerie had beat me out here by, what? maybe an hour?

I patted the smooth fender of my car, leaned against it. Finding the car brought me flush with cold reality. Until that moment all my energies had been focused on finding Valerie. Finding her physically, finding her mentally. Now I knew who she was, this adult child. I knew why she'd run away from paradise. And I knew where she was. Inside with the man who'd stolen her childhood.

I didn't know what to do about it.

Two hours earlier Valerie had told me she'd wouldn't go home, ever, except to get her little sister. Had she come to rescue Sherri? But two hours earlier Valerie hadn't known Geoff Reardon was dead.

I wondered if I should ring the doorbell of the house across the street, Jerry Toland's house, ask to use the phone, dial the police. I could hear myself trying to explain the uncomfortable urgency I felt.

I didn't go to Jerry Toland's house. I crept closer to

Valerie's, using my flashlight to guide me. Halfway up the walk a dark wrought-iron lamppost tried to trip me.

115 was a big, boxy Colonial with a two-car attached garage on the right, centered on maybe an acre of ground, painted a pale color with dark shutters. A stand of rhododendron bushes blocked the windows to the right of the door. The downstairs was dark, but lights blazed on the left side of the upper floor. I debated ringing the bell, skirted the path, and made my way closer to the lights.

The room underneath the lighted room was large, some kind of family affair, with leather couches, TV and stereo equipment, a patio, and sliding glass doors. A hooded barbeque grill blocked the center of the patio. A broad woodpile rose closer to the house. Even if I climbed the woodpile I couldn't reach that second-story room. Crouching near the sliding doors, I could hear noises. A man shouted something over a rhythmic thumping. There was another noise under the thumping but I couldn't make it out—a faint mewling, like a cat.

I tried the sliding doors but they were locked. I ran toward the front door, tripping over bushes. As I lifted my hand to ring the bell, all the lights in the house blackened. The noises disappeared. I froze with my hand raised.

Had Valerie used her key? Had she tried a secret approach?

I placed my hand on the front doorknob and carefully rotated it. It turned. I pushed the door and met with no resistance. Maybe Valerie had left it open to ease her later escape, once she'd found Sherri.

If she'd come back for her little sister.

The noises upstairs hadn't sounded like the successful result of a secret snatch-and-grab mission.

I patted my coat pocket and felt the reassuring metal, but I didn't take out my gun. I needed my right hand for the flashlight.

The beam showed me stairs, mounting to the left of the foyer, heavily carpeted. I took them well to the side, testing each one for creaks before committing my weight to it. While I climbed I worked out the geography of the house in my head. I was interested in the room with light, then with no light.

The second-floor foyer was carpeted with the same heavy stuff as the stairs. A skylight let in the stars so I could see four closed wooden doors. Two of them were on the left. Either could be the door to the room I wanted. I listened at the first. Nothing. I pressed up close to the second and heard ragged, labored breathing.

I turned the door handle gently, silently, holding my breath.

My flashlight showed a small room, a little girl's room with high shelves of dolls shadowing a single bed. A girl—Valerie by the clothing—lay across the bed, on top of the bedspread, tossed like a sack of laundry, knees drawn up, arms outflung. I thought she must be uncomfortable that way.

There was one window in the room, curtained. I crept closer to the bed, thinking I'd wake the girl, take her with me, to the police, to a therapist, somewhere safe.

"Valerie," I whispered.

Her breathing sounded wrong and I shone the light full on her face.

Blood trickled from one nostril. Her nose was smashed to one side and her face had the lumpy look a beating gives, before the bruises have a chance to color and the swelling to start. My jaw clamped shut and I ran my flashlight over a wider circle. A glass of water sat on her bedside table next to a bottle of pills.

I didn't pick them up, but I leaned closer to read the label. The prescription was for Mathilde Haslam. Serax, 30 MG. Take one before bedtime.

I touched a dark spot on Valerie's sweater. Not blood. Water. Her chin was damp too.

There was no phone in the room. I'd have to find a phone, dial 911.

The door to the room crashed open. Maybe the noise wasn't as loud as that, but I had my back to the door and the quiet, broken only by Valerie's attempts to breathe through her ruined nose, was so complete that the door, cracking against the opposite wall, sounded like thunder.

The overhead light blinked on, much too bright for my dark-adapted eyes. I squinted at the frilly pink room, filled with lace and dolls. The room of a small child. An immaculate child. Nothing out of place, not a china doll, not a stuffed animal. Except for the dark lump that was Valerie, bleeding on the bed.

Preston Haslam wore a bathrobe over slacks. His eyes behind the horn-rimmed spectacles were narrow, speculative.

"What's going on?" he said. "What are you doing here?" His voice was too loud, his face too red, his breathing too heavy.

"Your daughter stole my car," I said.

"I'm sorry," he said, striving for a smile, "but surely that can wait until morning."

"Your daughter can't," I said. "She needs a doctor."

"I don't think so," he replied, as if he'd given the matter careful consideration.

"Look at her," I said. "She's hurt."

"Yes," he said coolly. "She must have fallen on the stairs."

"She's out cold," I said.

"I think we should let her sleep," he said.

"There's a bottle of pills on the table. Your wife's sleeping pills."

"Yes," he said, "they are my wife's."

"Your daughter needs a doctor."

"No," he said.

"No?" I repeated, changing the inflection.

"Listen," he said. "You may think you're doing the right thing, but you don't know all the facts. My daughter's made a, uh, a choice and much as it hurts me, I think we have to respect her choice."

"Choice? Listen, buddy, call a doctor."

"My daughter has made her decision."

"What the hell are you talking about?" In the full overhead light Valerie's injuries looked worse. One of her eyes seemed swollen shut, one half-open. The pupil in the half-open eye was huge.

"I know you think you're doing the best thing for her," Haslam said firmly, "but she doesn't want to suffer anymore. She doesn't want the public shame, the embarrassment. She came home to tell me about it, to confess. I told her she'd always be my daughter, no matter what she did. But murder . . . she wanted this escape. Don't take it away from her."

I saw the whole setup in his triumphant eyes. Valerie was to take the blame. Again. With Valerie dead, an apparent suicide, any questions about Reardon's death were easy to answer. Even if no suspicion arose about Reardon's suicide he could still use it. He could say the drama teacher had been despondent about his daughter's disappearance. And Valerie had felt such guilt on hearing about his suicide that she'd chosen the same end.

Of course if anyone thought Reardon's death might be murder, well, here was Valerie tailor-made for the killer. Reardon had spurned her after promising to run off with her. She'd gone back to the Emerson, confronted him the day he died. She'd told Papa all about it, and much as he hated to sully his dead daughter's name, the truth was the best policy, wasn't it?

The cops knew how wild Valerie was. She had a history.

"So did she decide to kill herself before or after she fell down the stairs?" I said.

"What do you mean?"

"I mean the cops are going to ask you about that. About the beating. Your story is full of holes."

"Probably some pimp beat her up. Some lowlife she met in the Combat Zone. My daughter had a taste for that kind of thing, you know."

"I saw your daughter less than two hours ago. She had no marks on her face."

"So you say," Haslam replied. "So you say."

"Get this straight," I said. "Your daughter isn't going to suffer for you anymore."

"I don't think I understand you."

"Understand this. I'm taking your daughter out of here. With your help or without."

"You're an intruder in my house," he said.

"Don't worry. I won't stay long." I reached out a hand and touched Valerie's shoulder. She moaned and I said, "Valerie? Valerie, can you stand?" He couldn't have forced the pills on her more than fifteen minutes ago. I didn't know how quickly they'd take effect.

She moved and groaned and whispered, "Sherri?"

"We'll come back for Sherri," I promised. "First you have to come with me."

"Has my daughter been lying to you?" Haslam said confidently, leaning one shoulder against the door jamb. "I can see she has."

"No," I said. "She's been telling the truth."

"I doubt she knows what it means."

"We'll debate that later. Right now, call a doctor or get out of my way."

I stuffed my flashlight in my purse, slung it over my shoulder, leaned down, and picked up the girl, as gently as I could, like a baby, with one arm under her shoulders and one under her knees. She wasn't heavy, but her weight was dead in my arms. She didn't have the strength to hold on, to help in any way. She groaned, and, hearing it, I was glad. Even if the pain was bad, I was pleased she could still feel it. I didn't know how many of the pills she'd swallowed, how many had been forced down her throat.

I took a step toward the door. I'd carried heavier burdens, but not recently and not often.

It was a little gun, probably a .22. Haslam's fist almost smothered it.

"Put her down and get out," he said.

I stared at the gun for a moment, then backtracked, and obeyed. I don't think Valerie had any idea what was going on. She wasn't aware I'd picked her up. She wasn't aware I'd put her down.

I rested my hand near my right pocket.

"You have a big problem, Preston," I said.

"I'm not the one breaking and entering," he replied.

"Either I take your daughter with me or I call a doctor and wait until he comes. It's going to be hard to explain that you had to shoot me because I tried to get your kid to a doctor."

"Maybe Valerie shot you," he said with a smile. "She does such crazy things."

"Yeah," I agreed, "but do you know how to set that up? I mean you're an investment banker, not a cop." I stuck both hands in my pockets, casually. "Not a killer," I said.

"What do you mean, set it up?" he said. "I'll be an eyewitness. The police will believe me."

"It's tricky," I said. "You've got to think about powder burns, residue, things like that."

"I'll take the risk."

"Well, I hope the gun is licensed," I said.

"It's mine," he said. "Legally. Valerie must have stolen it. I had no idea she was so violent."

I thought I heard a faint noise across the hall, maybe a door opening.

"Of course, your wife might come in any minute," I said.

"My wife takes pills," he said. "She'll sleep through the Second Coming."

Footsteps crossed the rug. Behind Haslam I could see a small form, dark tousled hair, a sleepy disheveled face.

"Sherri," I said. "Run. Call the police. Tell them the house is on fire."

"Sherri," said her father. "You go right back to bed this instant."

The small child stuck a finger in her mouth, pivoted, and went back to bed. She even closed her door behind her.

Her obedience was unquestioning, unswerving. She'd listen to her father no matter what he told her to do. The thought of that tiny child and Preston Haslam made me breathe faster, made my eyes hurt.

My hand was in position now, finger poised.

"One," he said. He thought it was a game. Maybe he thought everyone would do what he wanted, like Sherri. Like Valerie used to do. Like his drugged wife.

"Two," he said softly, lining up the weapon, using both hands, as if a little .22 was going to have killer recoil.

I could almost trace the thoughts racing through his head. He didn't see any other way out, and I didn't wait for him to count three. No dramatic confrontation. No high noon. I didn't pull my gun and challenge him. I just shot him. Right through the fabric of my coat.

The .38 packs some recoil. I felt like my shoulder had been ripped off.

The bullet caught him high on the right side of the chest and spun him around. His hands scrabbled at the door frame and he came down heavily. He hardly made a noise on the thick carpet.

I walked over, my gun out of my pocket, pointed at

Haslam's head. He didn't look like he'd be going any-where, but I thought I'd better get his gun to make sure.

Leaning over him, I marveled at Sherri's closed door, the absolute lack of movement anywhere in the house, the absence of Mathilde Haslam. And I thought about what I'd told Haslam, about the cops and things being hard to explain. I put the safety on my gun, pulled on my right glove, and with his hand on the .22, I forced his finger to pull the trigger, firing a shot in the direc-tion I'd been standing only a moment ago. A second shot went a long way toward self-defense.

I felt the staggering pulse in his throat, saw the spreading stain on the carpet. I didn't think Haslam was going to be able to deny anything.

Valerie made a gagging noise and that brought me back. I stopped staring at the blood, at the man, and I raced down the hall, found a phone, dialed 911. I re-quested the police and two separate ambulances. Some-how it seemed important to me that daughter and father not have to travel in the same one.

My hand started shaking when I put the phone down, like some separate hand belonging to another body. I sat with Valerie until the ambulance arrived.

CHAPTER
33

Twenty-four hours after killing Preston Haslam, I was slumped in the passenger seat of an undercover cop car watching a three-story brick building on the corner of Huntington Avenue, near the Jamaicaway.

Joanne Triola, wearing a dark sweater and slacks, sat in the middle of the backseat. A blue-eyed rookie named O'Hara was on one side, a paunchy veteran filled the other. Both wore uniforms. Mooney was in the driver's seat.

Manelli was part-owner of the building, a fact turned up by carefully casual questioning of a fire department buddy. One of his cousins lived in apartment 3F.

Neighbors had mentioned the leggy blonde guest to Triola, who'd scouted the building in census-taker guise. Her man in Internal Affairs had more than lived up to expectation, forming a swift and secret unit to come to Mooney's aid. Triola said the guy's eyes glowed at the prospect of getting more goods on Manelli.

"Figure somebody tipped him off?" the rookie cop said, breaking a long silence.

"Which of us you think did it?" snapped the veteran.

"Cool it," said Triola.

"Hey," said the rook, "no offense. I meant the brass, you know, somebody high up—"

Triola said, "Probably you ought to keep your mouth shut."

That was one of the more civil exchanges of the past three hours. Tempers were running high, the way they usually do when the perpetrator about to be arrested is a cop.

Rain dotted the windshield. I watched a drop roll from top to bottom.

The two-way radio sputtered and came alive. Everyone tensed, but nothing happened.

"Look, Joanne, let me in on the bust," Mooney said, not for the first time.

"After the premises have been secured, we'll radio and you come up. That's the way it's planned and that's the way it's going down, Mooney."

"Dammit," he said. "I want to see the bastard when he realizes he's caught, when he sees what he's got himself into—"

"I understand, Mooney," Joanne said. "And if you

don't quit it, we're going home. Okay? You shouldn't be here at all."

I tapped him on the shoulder and gave him a warning glance. Joanne meant what she said.

The radio static died abruptly and so did the conversation. I closed my eyes, opened them. I didn't like what I saw with my eyes shut.

We sat in heavy silence for what seemed like days. Mooney's knuckles slowly whitened on the steering wheel.

The radio crackled and a tinny voice said, "We have target car approaching the area."

Joanne let out a breath. The rookie said, "Way to go."

"Shhhh," said the vet. It was hard to make out the words on the squawk box. The rookie patted his holster nervously.

"Target car is an '80 Nova, beige, proceeding north on Frawley, turning west corner of Huntington. . . ."

"That a boy," Mooney murmured, "keep comin' this way." I looked over at his face, what I could see of it in the streetlamp glow. I don't think he knew he'd spoken out loud.

We couldn't see the car approach. It was dark, but that wasn't the problem. Our unit was parked around the back of the building, shielded by a dumpster and a spreading tree. The two other units were even farther away. Nobody wanted to spook Manelli.

"Assume ready positions." The crackling order came after another five minutes of static.

"Go," Joanne said, and the two back doors eased open. "We'll call," she said to me and Mooney, especially to Mooney. "You stay put till then."

Mooney started to protest, stopped. The three cops melted into the darkness.

"You okay, Mooney?" I said.

"Yeah," he said. Then after a ten-count, "How about you?"

I shrugged. "I guess," I said.

"You wanna talk about what happened last night, the shooting—well, I'm here."

"Thanks."

We both watched raindrops for a while. Then I started talking, thinking I'd give him a short version of events at Valerie's house to make the time pass. I found my voice shaking when I got to the confrontation in the bedroom.

"Hey," Mooney said. "It's okay."

"It's just I can't believe I killed the guy. I mean, I remember the way the gun felt in my hand, but I don't remember deciding to shoot him. It happened so slowly—and it happened so fast."

"That's how it goes," he said. "And the wife never even woke up."

"She was like a kid herself, Mooney," I said. "Way younger than her husband. Not more than five-two. Tiny. Wearing baby doll pajamas, and drugged pretty well. She washed her sleeping pills down with scotch."

"Still—" Mooney said.

"Still what?" I said. "Still, she should have protected her daughter? Sure. But it wasn't her fault. Haslam's the one who raped his kid."

"Hey," Mooney said. "I never said different. Relax, okay?"

It was bad advice. When I relaxed I had trouble keeping my eyes open. When they closed I was back at Lilac Palace Drive.

I sat on the gray rug in Valerie's bedroom, my hand over hers, until the sirens wailed. Then I tried to stand up, but my knees and I decided against it. The door was open after all. The cops would find a way in.

"Up here," I yelled when I heard them enter, stumbling in the dark.

"I think he's dead," I said to the first man in the door, a white-coated paramedic. My teeth were chattering. I hadn't noticed how cold it was in the bedroom. "This one's been drugged and beaten. Needs her stomach pumped."

The man stopped at Preston Haslam's side.

"Take care of Valerie first," I said harshly. "This one first."

Then cops were everywhere.

Mrs. Haslam was so far under they had to take her along on a stretcher. And little Sherri—obedient, good, and scared—wouldn't come out of her room. Her dad had told her to stay there, and stay there she would. A policewoman had to go in for her.

"Where will they take her?" I asked.

The cop questioning me shrugged.

I said, "There are neighbors, the Tolands. They'd look after her."

"Address?" he said.

"Across the street."

"This is a nice area," the cop said. "Good people."

"Yeah," I said.

When questioned by the police, the idea is to answer politely, not spill your guts. Too much information confuses them. And if you start off by telling your story to some patrolman you have to tell it over and over up the ladder. I knew that so I resisted the impulse to blurt out the tale to the first sympathetic face. I waited until they got the chief of police out of bed.

When I showed him the extract from Valerie's diary, the atmosphere subtly changed. Once I explained how that tied Haslam into the Reardon suicide, the cops no longer looked at me as a disturber of the peace, killer of a respected citizen. They all looked like they wanted to cover their ears, their eyes, wash their hands.

"Do you have an officer who specializes in sexual trauma?" I asked.

"No," the chief said. "This isn't that kind of—"

"You ought to get a therapist over to the hospital," I said. "Valerie's going to need a good one."

The chief nodded to a younger man and he went out the door like he had a mission. I hoped he'd find someone who could help, someone gentle, someone who'd have the right words to tell Valerie that none of this was her fault. None of it . . .

"How's the girl?" Mooney asked, bringing me back.

"Who knows?" I said.

"It's funny," Mooney said.

"What?"

"All that time I spent looking for a blonde woman with a snake tattoo, and you say this Janine hasn't got any tattoos."

"She's a temporary tattoo girl, Mooney," I said. "Decals, like you used to stick on when you were a kid."

"Invisible tattoos," he said. "Yeah. Figures."

Invisible tattoos, I thought. Like the kind that drove Valerie from Lincoln to the Zone.

A metallic version of Joanne's voice said, "Come on up."

Mooney and I had the car doors open before her second word was out.

Apartment dwellers were hanging out into the hallway, staring at us wordlessly as we clattered up the two flights. Later, if we needed witnesses, the same tenants would swear they'd never stepped foot over their thresholds.

The door to 3F hung wide open. Inside you could tell there'd been a scuffle by the red faces and heavy breathing. The room was crowded with blue uniforms, six of them; the department was taking no chances on this one.

A cold breeze billowed the curtains. One of the windows was flung wide. Manelli—cuffed arms straining behind his back—must have tried to run for the fire escape.

Now he was busily trying to make amends for his instinctive flight, joking and winking with the cops, telling them an extramarital affair really didn't rate this kind of firepower. He saw Mooney and the jokes dried up.

When Mooney came through the door, the other cops fell back a step, leaving a clear path to Manelli. Mooney got within two feet of him and I tensed, ready for bloodshed. But Mooney just stood there, staring at him the way you'd look at a particularly loathsome slug.

"Get him out of here," Manelli said finally, lowering his eyes.

Janine recognized Mooney, too, no doubt about it. She wasn't cuffed, but Triola had her by the arm in a no-nonsense hold. The blonde made a quick choice.

"Hey," she said, "I just picked up the knife, that's all."

"Shut up," Manelli said.

"The hell I will. I mean, I thought I could use it. I gave it to this jerk," she nodded at Manelli, scorn dripping from her nasal voice, "when I saw the stuff in the papers. Figured he'd give me a break the next time I needed one, you know."

"Shut up," Manelli repeated.

"And instead of thank you very much, this bozo told me I'd rot in jail if I turned it in. I been rotting here," she said to Manelli, "I don't know what's the fucking difference."

"I don't know what the hell this bitch is talking about," Manelli said. "What knife?"

"Bastard," Janine said.

We read them their rights. That shut Manelli up, but Janine kept up her end of the conversation all the way down to headquarters.

CHAPTER
34

I didn't feel much like volleyball the next morning, but I forced my body through the motions and pretty soon the rhythm of the game took over, pulsing its urgent beat through my tired muscles: serve and return, spike and dig, setup, setup, over the net. My body loosened, my knee moved smoothly, and my mind woke to the rush of adrenaline. Kristy had a fine service game, and I got hot in the corner. We wound up aceing a tough inner-city Y team, and back in the locker room, panting and sweating, my hair soaked and my right arm practically dead, I was glad to be alive, glad I'd played.

I swam my twenty laps, showered, and dressed, then cut across the Mass. Ave. traffic to Dunkin' Donuts. I ordered two glazed doughnuts and coffee to go, and that's when I first realized I'd decided to visit Valerie in the hospital.

It was the first real spring day, the kind that said forget about winter, this is New England. The sun sparkled on tree branches that burst with tiny spearmint buds, the green new and fresh. I took off my sunglasses even though it meant squinting against the sun. I wanted the colors natural. My Toyota hummed, unharmed by its nighttime adventure, and I wound down the window and enjoyed the wind on my face.

Valerie was in Concord Hospital, a small well-endowed suburban place I'd never had occasion to visit. Still, a hospital is a hospital and the routine held. A plump lady at the front desk told me Valerie was in the A wing, Room 341. Take the elevators to the right.

I didn't inquire about visiting hours. She didn't tell me. I was there and I intended to visit.

Hospital beds diminish even the beefiest cops. Valerie looked tiny, half her age, tucked in the solemn whiteness of the mechanical bed. Her nose was completely hidden under white bandaging and plaster. Both eyes were black: deep, sunken, raccoon eyes. Her right cheek was rough and reddened, her left wrist immobilized with a cast.

Her eyes were closed. She wore no makeup. Without it, her face looked defenseless. I was glad someone had paid for a private room. I wondered who.

The TV was on, displaying some game show. The volume was off. If Valerie chose to open her eyes she could see smiling faces win and lose, brightly dressed Barbie dolls jump up and down.

I couldn't tell if she was asleep or resting. I stood by the bed a little while, waiting. The lashes fluttered.

"Hi," I said.

She gave no indication that she'd heard or seen me. Her eyes closed again.

"You okay?" I said.

"No," she said flatly, in such a quiet voice that I had to lean over to catch the monosyllable.

"Does your arm hurt? Want me to find a nurse who can give you something?"

Her eyes opened again, and her mouth moved in a humorless grimace. "Somebody who can knock me out for a million years, maybe," she said.

"Your nose doesn't look so hot, but it will. I broke my nose three times."

"Really?"

"Yep," I said.

For a minute I thought she might actually smile, but then her mouth shook and she whispered, "It's not my stupid nose."

"I know, Valerie."

"Sure." She pressed her lips tightly shut as if the one bitter word had escaped without her permission.

"I read your notebook."

"Shit," she said. "I mean, did Geoff pass it around? I mean, the cops and that shrink . . . Does everybody know about me?"

"No," I said. "No."

"It's not my nose or my arm or my teeth," she said. "If you read my stupid notebook, you know that. I wish to hell I'd never written it down, never passed it in—"

"Listen to me, Valerie. You didn't do anything wrong. Your father—" she winced when I said the word. I repeated it. "Your father did a terrible thing to you. But you didn't do anything wrong by telling."

"You don't understand—" she began, her voice getting louder, her cheeks reddening.

"Not unless you tell me," I agreed quietly.

She bit her lower lip with her teeth and closed her eyes. I waited until she opened them. "He was my dad," she said, haltingly at first, then picking up speed. "And I loved him. You know. I wanted him to be happy—" Her voice dropped to a whisper. "And what you ought to know about me, what everybody ought to know—is that sometimes I wanted it. I mean, I enjoyed it. It was like being better than my mom, and he depended on me—so it's not like I'm normal or anything—I *asked* for it, and it's my fault he's dead—"

"How old were you, Valerie? When it started?"

"I don't remember," she murmured. "When I was real little he'd just, you know, just touch me. And he'd say how good I felt, and how much he loved me, and how special I was. And how Mommy was sick and I could help her by being the secret Mommy. But it had to be our special secret. I could never, never tell."

"Valerie, you were a child. You had no choice—"

"Later, I didn't want to. I didn't want him to get on top. It hurt, and I knew it wasn't right, but he loved me so much—and now he's dead and it's my fault—"

"No," I said firmly, trying to catch her eye, to hold it, to burn the words home. "Don't ever say that. Don't ever think that, Valerie."

I put my hand over hers the way I had while we

waited for the ambulance, and she cried, tears running unchecked down her face, sliding into the white pillows under her head.

"And then there's Geoff," she said, gulping through her tears. "Geoff tried to help me and—" She was off on a fresh round of sobbing. I found a box of tissues and handed them to her.

When she'd composed herself a little I asked, "You want a glass of water or anything?"

"No," she said. "I didn't mean to cry."

"It's okay," I said.

"It's like all I do." She wadded used tissues in her hands. "All I do is cry."

"It's okay," I repeated. Then after a long pause, punctuated by her sniffles and gulps, I said, "If you want to, talk about Geoff, that's okay, too."

"What about him?"

"Anything," I said. "Anything you want to tell me."

"Did you know him?"

"I met him," I said.

"He was so handsome, wasn't he?" she said, staring at the television screen. "And he always wanted us to talk to him, to tell him stuff, to tell him secrets and stuff, things we wouldn't tell anybody else. He had a game we used to play in class, a truth game, where you'd have to tell something truthful about yourself, something you'd never told anybody before. He said it would build trust, you know."

"Yeah," I said.

"I liked him. He seemed so, you know, interested in me, like he could see something in me that nobody else could."

How attractive that must have been, I thought. Being special to a man who looked like Geoffrey Reardon.

"I couldn't say anything about, you know, *anything* in class," she said. "I wouldn't, but more and more, I'd think about telling him, and then I wrote it in my notebook. I wasn't gonna pass it in. I just wrote it. I don't know what I was thinking. And then he said I'd fail if I didn't hand it in right then, and I just did. It was like I couldn't stand it anymore. I needed him to know. But then I couldn't face him—"

"So you ran away."

"Yeah."

I said, "You ran away because of Jerry Toland, too, right? Because he kissed you?"

"I thought he was my friend, but—"

"He hired me to find you."

"Not my—my, uh, dad?"

"No."

"Oh," she said.

"A lot of people care about you, Valerie," I said.

"I got Geoff killed," she said. "That's my fault, too." Her words came out in a low flat whisper. She wasn't crying, but her chest shook. She probably didn't have any tears left.

I thought about Geoff Reardon, urging his students' confidences, expecting nothing he couldn't handle. I wondered how he justified his prying. Once he got his students to tell their stories, to own up to their truths, what did he expect? If a kid fell apart under the weight of all that knowledge, did he know how to put her back together again? Or was he practicing psychiatry without a license?

Like me.

"Your father killed Geoff Reardon," I said. "You had no control over what your father did."

"I got my father killed."

"But it was never your fault. Not for the tiniest moment. Not for one second. You did the right thing. You had to tell somebody." I wished that Reardon had handled her confidence differently, gone straight to some school psychologist. . . .

"Valerie," I went on when she didn't say a thing, "let me use a real cornball word here. You know what you are? You're a hero."

"Heroine," she said.

"Nah," I said. "It always sounds watered down that way. You went back to that house to rescue your little sister. You protected her from your father. You're a hero. A secret hero if that's the way you want it to be, but a hero."

"I don't want to be a stupid hero."

"I know," I said. "But sometimes you don't get a choice."

A nurse came in with orange juice and a hypo, and asked me what I thought I was doing. Visiting hours had not yet begun and I would have to leave immediately. She was of the old school, immaculately white-clad, her cap rigged at battle tilt. Not a woman to trifle with.

"I'll be back, Valerie," I promised, squeezing her good right hand.

Tears were running down her cheeks and I'm not sure she heard me. I hoped they were cleansing tears, but I knew she needed more help than I could give her, help for the rest of her life.

CHAPTER
35

Mooney dropped by about eight that evening, in time to catch the Twin Brothers on their way out. I was actually shaking their hands, congratulating them on a job well done—uttering words of praise I thought would never pass from my lips to their ears. Roz, her hair a strange new shade of orange, was beaming.

"Great job," I said to Rodney. "Really."

"Sorry about the, uh, water damage—" George said.

"Yeah, well," I said, "no sweat. Get your truck fixed."

That's when Mooney pounded up the walk and rang the bell and put an end to our fond farewells. He was wearing full-dress uniform and it took Roz and the boys by surprise.

"Hi," he said. "You busy?"

Roz went out to the truck with the brothers who suddenly remembered an urgent need to depart. Cop uniforms affect a lot of people that way. Roz was murmuring something about throwing an "opening" for the bathroom. I'd already vetoed the idea.

"Come on in," I said to Mooney. "How'd the hearing go?"

"Not bad," he said.

"Yeah?" I smiled with real pleasure. Mooney's voice was back to its normal growl, the tightness gone. He looked as if he'd lost ten pounds and five years.

"That Janine was some witness," he said.

"Talkative?"

Mooney said, "Seems like Manelli and Janine had a thing going. She knew he was on the outs with me, because of the bar scam and all, and when she saw the fight, she thought of a way to make Manelli happy. Thought he'd be grateful."

"And he was," I said.

"Yeah. He was protecting the Blue Note so he didn't have any trouble shutting up the regulars there. But Janine figured she'd done enough. She didn't want to stay incommunicado for months while the cops searched for her. She wanted to work. Manelli wouldn't let her and she was pissed. And an angry witness—"

"Is a good witness," I finished. "Want to sit down?"

"Sure," he said. "You had dinner?"

"I think so," I said. "Tell the truth, I'm not sure."

I sank into Aunt Bea's rocker for the second time in a week. Maybe I was getting used to the fact that she wasn't going to need it again. Mooney tried the couch and T.C. came over and sniffed his well-polished shoe with some disdain. T.C. is not crazy about Mooney. It's that competitive thing he has with other males.

"How's the girl doing?" Mooney asked.

I shrugged.

"Does she know about Reardon?" he asked.

"Well," I said, "yes and no. She knows he's dead. She knows her dad probably killed him. The Lincoln police sent some fibers and hairs and stuff to the State Lab, evidence that proves Haslam was in Reardon's car. She doesn't know that Reardon tried to help her by blackmailing her dad. I mean, she may have to know someday, but not now. As far as I'm concerned, she needs to believe that somebody stood up for her—"

"Yeah," Mooney said. "The truth will set you free."

"How free?" I said.

"Speaking of free." He reached over and scratched behind T.C.'s ears. "I'll bet you didn't deposit my check."

"Ah, Mooney," I said. "Do we have to start this again?"

T.C. rumbled, his version of a purr.

"Look," Mooney said, "you found her. I owe you."

"Forget it, Mooney."

"Did you get paid for finding Valerie?"

"Two checks in the mail this morning," I said. "And guess who wrote one?"

"The father?"

"Nope. No hands from the grave on this one. The mother. Mathilde Haslam."

"Good for her," Mooney said. "At least she did something. She send a note or anything?"

"Nope," I said. "I mean, what could she say?"

"Yeah," Mooney said. "Well, money talks."

"Agreed."

"She pay well?"

"Very, and then I got a check from Jerry, the kid who hired me in the first place. His family's taking care of Valerie's little sister. Just when I think I've got it straight—all people are rotten—somebody comes along and proves me wrong."

"Keeps you off balance," Mooney said.

"Yeah, well, between the two checks, I ought to be able to add a little to Paolina's college fund. And since I found Janine while I was looking for Valerie, consider me paid."

"It doesn't feel right," he said. "But thanks."

"You're welcome," I said, and I tried to get him to join me in a smile.

"The Vietnamese guy?" I guessed when he didn't respond.

"Yeah," he said. "I was just over there, at the hospital."

"And?"

"The wife doesn't blame me. Poor kid. She blames herself."

"And the doctors?"

"Doctors," Mooney said, the way he might say "bookies" or "thieves." "What the hell do they really know?"

"The guy's alive, Mooney," I said. "Alive is a good sign."

"Yeah," he muttered. "I guess." He loosened his regulation tie, yanked the knot down about five inches, and opened the top button of his uniform shirt.

"Beer?" I asked.

"In a minute."

"Thought much about staying on the force?" I asked.

"It's all I think about," he said.

"Give it a chance, Moon," I said. "Who knows? You might like it."

"And besides," he said, poker-faced, "I have so many other marketable skills."

"Mooney," I said after a while. "You ever shoot anybody and not feel bad about it?"

"I haven't shot a lot of people," he said. "Thank God."

"I keep thinking about Haslam. The man was sick, to do that to his own child, but—"

"Yeah," Mooney said. "But."

"I hate thinking I killed some guy who couldn't help doing what he did. But dammit, what he did was so wrong—and Valerie was so goddamned defenseless—"

"Carlotta," Mooney said. "At least for the girl's sake, it's probably better he's dead."

"You think so?"

"Think about the trial," he said. "Shit."

"Yeah." I hadn't told Mooney about firing Haslam's gun. The Lincoln cops hadn't questioned the shootout story.

"Hey," I said. "You want that drink now?"

"Sure," he said, tailing me into the kitchen.

"What the hell happened?" he said, as soon as he looked around.

"Oh, you mean the ceiling?"

"Yeah," he said.

"The plumbers," I said.

"The guys who left when I came in?"

"Yeah."

"They looked familiar."

"Friends of Roz," I said.

"Looks pretty bad." He stared up at the peeling paint.

"Well, yes and no," I said. "It's all fixed. I've just gotta scrape it and paint it. Roz volunteered to do it, except I'm afraid she'll paint the ceiling black or something. I was pretty upset when it happened, but they did an absolutely terrific job upstairs. New tub, new sink. Roz designed it, and damn if it isn't gorgeous."

"This I have to see," Mooney said.

"Okay," I said. "Bring your beer."

Mooney's never been upstairs in my house before. I wasn't sure if it was a good precedent, but, really, I was so damned pleased about the bathroom I only gave it a passing thought.

Roz had been right. The chocolate tile was perfect. The Day-Glo orange sink, the one with the busted faucet, had disappeared to my delight, and been replaced with a beige pedestal sink, sleek and modern. All the fixtures were shades of beige—"almond," "toast," and "wheat" if memory served—and none of them quite matched. But Roz had brought them all together with paint. She'd done this thing with the walls—she called it a stippled faux-marbre effect—with different shades of beige and pink and gold, that made all the different fixtures look like they'd been planned just the way they were.

And the tub was great. Not a Jacuzzi or anything fancy, but a tub big enough to stretch out in. I had a bottle of Caswell-Massey Lily of the Valley Bubble Bath perched on its side, and plans to dedicate the tub that night. I hadn't quite decided whether to christen it alone or call Sam to help me. I was tired, but maybe not that tired.

"Pretty snazzy," Mooney said.

Roz had painted the ceiling pink. Pink is not my favorite color, but it gave the room a cheerful glow.

I guess I'd just expected Mooney to give the room a perfunctory glance and an approving noise, but he pushed over to the sink and inspected it in a professional way. Then he checked the toilet, eyeing the label. And then he sat down on the edge of the tub, started to say something, and wound up laughing.

"Well, I don't think it's so funny," I said.

"Oh, yes you will," he said, trying to regain his composure.

"Come on downstairs." I figured the strain of the hearing had finally gotten to him. "Drink your beer."

"You'd better drink yours," he said, chuckling madly and hanging onto the banister on the way down.

"Why?"

"Because you've got more trouble than you think," he said.

We sat at the kitchen table. I took a deep breath and said, "What's wrong? Did they do something to the main drain?"

"Nope," he said.

"Then what? Why are you giggling like a moron?"

"Is one of the guys named Rodney?" he asked.

"Yeah," I replied slowly.

He took a big gulp of beer. "Carlotta, listen. I don't know a good way to tell you this. You got a bathroom full of stolen appliances up there."

"No."

"Yeah, Carlotta. Honest. All that stuff fell off the back of a truck, you know what I mean?"

"I'll kill them," I said.

"Shit, Carlotta. I just saw the report."

"Oh my God, Mooney. You're kidding."

"I swear I'm not."

I drank some beer. I couldn't taste it. "Is this receiving stolen property or what?"

"It could be," he said through another fit of giggles. I've never known Mooney to giggle.

"Could be," I repeated.

"I don't have to say anything," he said. "You could pretend I never went upstairs."

"Mooney, let me get this straight. You mean for the rest of my life I'll have to worry about who uses my bathroom? Maybe put up a sign: No cops in the bathroom."

"It'd be easy to let it go," he said. "Except—"

"Oh, Mooney," I said. "You don't tell on me. I don't tell on you, and pretty soon we're like Manelli, right?"

"Well," he said. "Not that bad."

I drank beer. I could feel a fit of the giggles coming on. Or maybe tears. "But that's what it would be, Mooney. I'd have to live with it. This would be your favor to me—and then I'd owe you one—and then—hell."

"It's not a capital crime," Mooney said.

"What is? Getting a little kickback from a bar? Being afraid to tell your mom or your teacher what your dad did to you after school? Looking the other way when your husband and your daughter spend a little too much time together? How does it start, Mooney? With somebody shutting his eyes, shutting her eyes, letting it go this one time. Once you start letting things go—"

"Come on, Carlotta, aren't you getting a little over-wrought about this?"

"Yeah," I said, teeth clenched, "I am."

"I'm really sorry, Carlotta," he said. But he couldn't quite keep a straight face.

"Dammit," I said.

"It'd look better if you called it in," Mooney said. "Good defense against receiving."

"Christ, Mooney, they'll take the stuff as evidence, right? They'll take my bathtub. I have got to have a bath, Mooney. I mean I'm desperate."

"Well, I've got a solution," he said.

"Yeah," I said, "I'll bet you do."

"Look, you're probably hungry, right? We could go out and get something to eat. Ice cream, if that's all you want. Herrell's or anyplace you want. And my mom's visiting her cousin. I have a tub. Nothing real special, but a tub."

"Mooney," I said warily, "you didn't know about this before?"

"Huh? What do you mean? I just thought I recognized the guy on the way out. Rodney what's-his-name."

"And you're not pulling my leg?"

"I wouldn't do that. The stuff is hot, Carlotta. I'm not saying you knew about it. I'm not saying Roz knew about it, but she's got rotten taste in friends."

All the time Mooney was talking I had the image of cops dancing in my head, cops ripping my brand-new bathroom apart. It was practically unbearable so I switched channels.

I thought about Sam Gianelli and his dark wavy hair

and his Charles River Park apartment and his wonderful sunken bathtub. Then I looked over at Mooney—solid, substantial Mooney. Maybe if he hadn't been wearing the uniform. . . .

"Sorry, Mooney," I said. "I've got other plans for tonight."